SO-AKQ-168

OTHER YEARLING BOOKS YOU WILL ENJOY:

FOOTSTEPS ON THE STAIRS, *C. S. Adler*
THE HAUNTING OF CASSIE PALMER, *Vivien Alcock*
THE GRIFFIN LEGACY, *Jan O'Donnell Klaveness*
THE TALKING TABLE MYSTERY, *Georgess McHargue*
THE TURQUOISE TOAD MYSTERY, *Georgess McHargue*
THE HEADLESS CUPID, *Zilpha Keatley Snyder*
THE FAMOUS STANLEY KIDNAPPING CASE, *Zilpha Keatley Snyder*
THE TRUTH ABOUT STONE HOLLOW, *Zilpha Keatley Snyder*
BLAIR'S NIGHTMARE, *Zilpha Keatley Snyder*
THE EGYPT GAME, *Zilpha Keatley Snyder*

YEARLING BOOKS/YOUNG YEARLINGS/YEARLING CLASSICS are designed especially to entertain and enlighten young people. Charles F. Reasoner, Professor Emeritus of Children's Literature and Reading, New York University, is consultant to this series.

For a complete listing of all Yearling titles,
write to Dell Readers Service,
P.O. Box 1045, South Holland, IL 60473.

SIZZLE AND SPLAT

Ronald Kidd

A YEARLING BOOK

Published by
Dell Publishing
a division of
The Bantam Doubleday Dell Publishing Grc
666 Fifth Avenue
New York, New York 10103

The trademark Yearling® is registered in the U.S. Patent and Trademark Office.

ISBN: 0-440-47970-3

Reprinted by arrangement with Lodestar Books, E. P. Dutton

Printed in the United States of America

November 1986

10 9 8 7 6 5 4 3

CW

to Russ Kidd and Tony Plog

Prelude

██░██░██░██

"Splat?"

"Huh?"

"What happened? I can't see a thing."

"Either we were swallowed by a whale, or we're dining in an exceptionally intimate restaurant."

"Somebody hit me over the head."

"That does it! I'm calling the maitre d'."

"Will you stop kidding around? Somebody must have knocked us out and thrown us in this room, or whatever it is. We've got to get out before they come back."

"You're right. I'm sorry."

"That's more like it. Now let's get going."

"Okay. Waiter, our check, please."

1

![checkered bar decoration]

The man looked like Santa Claus.

Oh, there were other ways of describing him. You could say that his eyes danced and sparkled, or that his cheeks looked like twin scoops of strawberry ice cream, or that his flowing beard was not gray, or even silver, but snow white. You could say that his stomach looked as round and comfortable as a beanbag chair, or that his grin peeked through the beard like a child playing hide-and-seek. But the truth was, Hans Kleiman looked like he should be flying through the night behind a team of the North Pole's finest—and I don't mean the Arctic police force, unless they've started recruiting guys with antlers.

The fact that he looked like Santa was ironic when you consider the gift he left us—the gift that started the break-ins and threats and lootings and kidnappings and high-speed car chases, to say nothing of my close encounters of the weird kind with possibly the most disgusting person ever to place his lips on the mouthpiece of a tuba. The gift that, in the end, turned out to be worth every bit of trouble, and more.

But on that first day, I didn't know about the gift. All I knew was that the man standing in the doorway looked like Santa Claus.

"Well, well, well," he chuckled, peering at the four of us on his front doorstep, "what have we here?" He spoke with an accent, giving his *w*'s a *v* sound. His gaze brushed each of us in turn until it came to rest on the nervous fifty-year-old man at the back of the group. "Oh, Buckminster. What is it you want?"

Buckminster Brody cleared his throat and wiggled his eyebrows. "Well, you see, Uncle Hans, we're here to find out, that is, we're here to inquire—we're here to *ask* whether you could do a favor for us, a very great favor. Could we—might we—come in for a moment?"

"Why, yes, certainly." Kleiman led us through the entry-way into a drawing room that belonged in eighteenth-century England, not twentieth-century Los Angeles. It was paneled in wood and furnished with antiques, including a vintage harpsichord in one corner. But the thing you really noticed was its size. The place was huge, probably bigger than the entire apartment where my dad and I lived.

"Didn't they play last year's Super Bowl here?" I whispered to Brody—at least, I thought I had whispered.

"They were going to," said Kleiman, "but the floors were too slippery. Too bad—I had the peanut concession. Tell me, young lady, are you a football fan?"

"I've been known to diagram a pass play or two."

"Prudence, please," said Brody. "Uncle Hans, we're here

representing the Pirelli Youth Orchestra. Allow me to introduce the group. The young woman you've been speaking to is Prudence Szyznowski."

"You can call me Sizzle," I said. "It sounds better."

Kleiman grinned. "Sizzle. I like that. And you may call me Hans."

"Miss Szyznowski is our principal trumpet player and chairman, that is, chairperson, of our musicians' steering committee." Brody indicated an immaculately groomed young man wearing an ascot. "This is our vice-chairman and concertmaster, Anthony Formica."

"Mr. Brody," said Anthony, "you know very well it's pronounced Formeeca, as in *me.*" He swiveled neatly on one heel and toe. "Mr. Kleiman, it's a great, great privilege. I've admired your music for years. And by the way, you may call me Anthony." He held out his hand.

Kleiman gripped it briefly. "You," he replied, smiling back, "may call me Mr. Kleiman."

"And this gentleman," Brody went on, "is someone whose name I'm sure you will know, that is, recognize. . . . He's Maestro Vidor Pirelli, founder and conductor of the orchestra."

"Yes, of course, maestro," said Kleiman. "I've heard much about your orchestra. Unfortunately, my health has prevented me from hearing it in person."

Pirelli, a swarthy man with a bright smile and a hook nose, bobbed quickly in his version of a gracious bow. He and Brody, between the two of them, had enough nervous energy to light a city the size of Pittsburgh. "The pleasure is for me, Mr. Kleiman," he blurted in his curious, unidentifiable accent.

Kleiman motioned for us to sit down. "So, Buckminster, to what do I owe the pleasure of this visit?"

4

It sounded strange to hear somebody address Buckminster Brody by his first name. It wasn't that he was such a dignified person; it was just that if you started out calling him Buckminster, you might later be tempted to shorten that to Bucky, and that wouldn't go over too well with either Brody, his dentist, or the Society for the Prevention of Cruelty to Beavers. The fact was that Buckminster Brody had the two biggest front teeth this side of the San Diego Zoo.

Brody fiddled with his tie. "Uncle Hans, I'll get right to the heart of the matter. The Pirelli Youth Orchestra is in serious, that is, grave, financial trouble. We get some help each year from the musicians' union trust fund, but these days that doesn't go very far. We've limped by for the past year now on a very limited budget, and I'm afraid that finally our cash flow has reached a point, that is, our situation is perilously close to . . ."

"We're broke," I said.

"Mm, yes, I see," Kleiman replied.

"As president of the orchestra association," Brody continued, "I've met with the steering committee, which you see before you, and we've decided to give a benefit concert to raise capital, I mean, funds. . . ."

"Money," I said.

"Ah," murmured Kleiman, nodding.

Brody leaned forward. "I'll lay it right on the line, Uncle Hans. We were hoping, that is, we wondered if it's possible . . ."

"We'd like you to write a piece for the concert," I said. "It would be a world premiere, and lots of people would come to hear it, and we'd make enough money to keep going for another year."

"Something like that," Brody mumbled.

5

Anthony beamed. "Feel free to write a violin concerto, Mr. Kleiman. As you may know, I'm about to launch a solo career, and nothing would please me more than to premiere a new Kleiman composition."

"Anthony," said Pirelli, "perhaps we must be letting Mr. Kleiman decide for himself." He turned to the composer and continued at his usual breathless pace. "Please excuse our Anthony. Sometimes he talk with his tongue too much. We would be proud to having you write even just a small piece for us. And we shall be understanding if you can't do this."

All of us studied Hans Kleiman for clues as to what he would decide. It occurred to me that the future of the orchestra was probably hanging in the balance.

He tugged at his beard. He scratched behind one ear. He laced his fingers together and brought them up to his chin.

"Sizzle," he said, "do you play Monopoly?"

2

Does Baryshnikov dance? Does O. J. Simpson run? Does Johnny Carson smirk?

My dad and I had played Monopoly once a week for the past four years, ever since my mom left. I'm not saying I was good, but usually I gave my dad Boardwalk and Park Place at the start of each game just to even things up.

"I've tried it a few times," I answered. "Why?"

"Would you like to play a game right now?"

The others seemed as confused as I was, except for Brody, who wore the look of a man sentenced to five years watching vacation slides. "I guess so," I said.

"Wonderful! Just follow me." Kleiman led us out of the drawing room, through a series of arched hallways, and down a narrow winding stairway. At the bottom he opened a door, and we entered a room at least twice as big as the first. But the items that filled it were hardly antiques. The place was a game player's dream.

One entire wall was lined with pinball machines. Another wall had enough video games to keep a thirteen-year-old kid busy until he qualified for Social Security. At one end was a shuffleboard court, over which hung a dart board. Scattered through the rest of the room were tables piled with games of every description. I saw Clue, Risk, checkers, Boggle, Parcheesi, Pit, Scrabble, backgammon, Yahtzee, chess. There were crossword puzzles, acrostics, word searches, and cryptograms. And there were jigsaw puzzles—some in boxes, some finished, and some half-finished. In front of one sat an elderly gray-haired woman wearing a red print dress and a big smile. I knew it could be none other than Mrs. Claus.

"Hello, Aunt Frieda," said Brody. Watching them embrace warmly, I remembered his telling me they were like mother and son, the only surviving relatives on his mother's side of the family.

"I'm Frieda Kleiman," she said to the rest of us, with only the slightest hint of a German inflection, "and as you can see, my husband loves games."

"I myself designed this room," the composer said. "It used to be a storage area, but we added wood paneling, carpets, and plenty of lights, since there are no windows. Other than a few special features, the room is very simple and has but one purpose: to give us a place to enjoy our games."

I pointed to an item that seemed out of place: the grand piano in the corner. "I suppose you play air hockey on that," I said.

He shook his head. "Tiddlywinks."

"You play tiddlywinks on a Steinway?" Anthony asked.

"Yes, I tried a Baldwin, but the surface wasn't right. The tiddlies kept slipping off the winks."

"Do you ever compose on it?" asked Mr. Pirelli.

"Certainly. That is the main reason I have it down here. Music, you see, is the greatest game of all."

"Speaking of which . . ." Brody ventured.

"But enough about the room—we have a Monopoly game to play." Kleiman led us over to a nearby table and motioned for me to sit down opposite him. "Guests go first."

I threw the dice, and the game was underway. I followed what I like to call my Conrad Hilton strategy: If it moves, build a hotel on it. Kleiman kept pace, watching me closely.

For the first fifteen minutes or so the others looked on, but as the match inched its way toward the half-hour and then the hour mark, they drifted off to games of their own. Soon Anthony had his head buried in a book of crossword puzzles, and Brody and Pirelli were engrossed in a frenzied round of Pac-Man.

As I went into hock to buy St. Charles Place, Kleiman said, "You know, I can tell a lot about people by the way they play games. You, for example, like to make quick decisions and take chances. You're impulsive, are you not?"

"That's what my dad tells me, but then he doesn't even like to shave without getting three estimates."

"I would also say you have a great deal of self-confidence. And obviously you enjoy winning."

"Who doesn't?"

"You might be surprised. For many years my wife would purposely let me win, because she wanted to see me happy. Now, however, she knows that what I like best is to have a good, hard-fought game. This is not to say that I enjoy losing. But, Sizzle, it is the *possibility* of losing that makes

9

winning worthwhile. In other words, if you cannot lose, you cannot really win, either. Or to put it another way, losing is what makes winning fun."

He counted out three thousand dollars and placed hotels on Pacific, North Carolina, and Pennsylvania avenues. "Think of the rose, Sizzle. It has a lovely life, but a very short one. When we inhale its fragrance, we enjoy it more because we know it will be gone in a few days. If it lasted forever, somehow it would not be so beautiful. Roses die, and people die, too. We die that we may live; we lose that we may win."

After a moment I threw the dice, and my token came to rest on Pennsylvania Avenue. "That will be fourteen hundred dollars, please," Kleiman said.

There was a sinking feeling in the pit of my stomach. I knew I had overextended myself. I tried selling hotels and mortgaging every property I owned but still came up a hundred dollars short.

"I hate to lose," I mumbled.

"Remember what I told you, Sizzle."

Kleiman got to his feet. "And now I have news that may cheer up all of you." The others left their games and scurried over. "Ladies and gentlemen, I have decided to compose a piece for your upcoming concert."

All around, there were excited grins. "Mr. Kleiman," Pirelli blurted, "we are so grateful, so grateful indeed."

"And I have decided something else. The piece will be a concerto, to be premiered by one of the members of your orchestra."

Anthony jumped to his feet. "A violin concerto! Thank you, sir!"

"No, not a violin concerto," Kleiman said. He flashed me a Santa Claus smile. "I will compose a trumpet concerto."

3

At the top of the blackboard were three words: *desire, discipline, dedication*. Below them were hundreds of *x*'s chalked into neat rows, columns, and formations. The figure pacing back and forth in front of the blackboard might have been Vince Lombardi or Knute Rockne, except as far as I know, neither wore lipstick or had his nails done at Elizabeth Arden's. The figure, all four feet ten of her, was Donna Kelly, director of the Westside High School marching band.

"We lost some key players last year," she said. "Roberts went to USC, Clark and Cohen went to UCLA, Jefferson went to Purdue, plus dozens of rank-and-file members either graduated or didn't sign up for this season. We've got a tough schedule coming up against some of the best bands in southern California, and it's going to take an all-out effort by everyone here to beat them."

It was the first rehearsal of the school year, a full month since the visit with Hans Kleiman. Two hundred kids were jammed into the Westside High band room. The place was so hot you could have fried an egg on the snare drum.

But it didn't seem to bother Miss Kelly. While the rest of us sweltered in jeans and short sleeves, she wore wool skirts and sweaters and somehow managed to stay as cool as the Minnesota Vikings in January. Only her pep talks were heated.

"If you remember the three *d*'s," she exhorted, "we'll be able to plug up the holes, cut our losses, and emerge with flying colors."

I gave a low whistle of admiration and made three more marks in my notebook. It had been a brilliant speech, even by Miss Kelly's high standards. She had been talking for less than an hour, and already she had racked up a near record 287 clichés—3 in the last sentence alone. Rumor had it that over the summer she took private lessons with Horace "Plat-itude" Potter, a local football announcer and acknowledged king of clichés.

"I think that about wraps it up for today," she said. "Next time, I'll be filling you in on the details of our game plan. In the meantime, if you have any questions, my door is always open. You're dismissed."

I circled the final total of 290 at the top of the page and closed my notebook. Grabbing my trumpet case, I rose and began shouldering my way toward the door and fresh air, but before I got halfway there I heard my name called.

"Szyznowski, could you come here for a minute?" It was Miss Kelly. Fighting the current, I moved back toward the blackboard, where I found her standing next to a scrawny

12

creature whose appearance was dominated by a mop of greasy hair. "Szyznowski, I wonder if you could do me a favor. This fellow's transferring in as a senior, and he's interested in finding out about youth orchestras in the area. I told him it was out of my bailiwick but right up your alley, and that you could give him a line on the situation."

I responded in terms she could understand. "You can count on me, Miss Kelly. No sooner said than done." I turned to the new arrival. "It's pretty hot in here. Let's go outside."

I led the way through the door to a shady bench. "So what's your name?" I asked.

He pushed the stringy hair out of his eyes, revealing a prominent forehead, hollow cheeks, a beaklike nose, and a crooked mouth set off by a complexion that in some places resembled the lunar surface and in others a pizza with everything on it. He was about average height, but his sticklike arms and a caved-in chest gave him a decidedly wimpy air. He wore faded jeans and an oil-stained T-shirt bearing the words *Mahler grooves*. In the midst of it all, his eyes danced a fractured samba.

"My name," he answered in a rich baritone voice, "is Arthur Hadley Reavis Pauling the Third. But my intimates prefer to avoid that exceedingly awkward appellation by employing my nickname. You, madame, may do the same."

"What's your nickname?"

"Splat."

"Splat?"

"Splat."

"How did you get a name like that?"

"In point of fact, it derives from a particularly turbulent period of my youth. I had neither siblings nor friends, so I would run about causing mischief. My favorite activity was

13

capturing plump toads in the bog behind our house, then carrying them to the street, where I would hurl them into the air as high as I could. The poor devils couldn't help but come down. Gravity, you know."

"Oh my God."

"The name, like the toads, stuck."

"That's disgusting."

He smiled and nodded, and then suddenly he began to laugh. This was no ordinary laugh. It was the shriek of a crazed hyena, a piercing reminder that it hadn't been too many years since people moved around on all fours and cringed at the sight of fire. Instinctively I drew away from him, and the shriek became a high-pitched cackle. As he laughed, he rocked back and forth, clapping his hands feebly with what little motor control his seizure had left him. After a few moments, the cackling dwindled to a low giggle, and he wiped his eyes with the backs of his hands. "Hey, that was great," he wheezed.

"Are you done?" I asked.

"Um-hm."

"Do you always act like this?"

He primped his Pennzoil perm. "Only when I'm trying to impress someone."

"Is that what you were doing?"

"In my own twisted way, yes. But enough about me. Let's talk about Mahler."

"You really want to know about youth orchestras?"

"You got it, chum."

"It's hard to picture you playing Mahler or anything else. What's your instrument?"

He made a futile effort to swell his concave chest. "Tuba—or as I like to call it, the tubaphone. What do you

14

play? And while you're at it, what was your name again?"

"I play the trumpet." I hesitated. I always hesitate before telling people my name. "I'm Prudence Szyznowski, but everyone calls me Sizzle. I'd advise you to do the same." I tried to look menacing, which was made easier by the fact that at five feet eleven I loomed several inches above my T-shirted tormentor.

He smiled up at me, unaffected. "You're cute when you do that," he said.

"Cute!" There are many things in the world I don't like to be called, but of all of them, *cute* is in capital letters at the top of the list. "Has anyone ever poured Drano down your tuba?" I inquired.

"Ooh, I love it when you talk like that."

"You're impossible."

"As Miss Kelly would say, you've hit the nail on the head."

"Hey, look, Splat the Third or whatever your name is, I'm supposed to meet my dad at four o'clock. Is there something specific you want to know, or are you just trying to recruit people to join you in your padded cell?"

"Actually, both. But for now just tell me about that orchestra."

"It's called the Pirelli Youth Orchestra. You've got to be pretty good to join, though."

"I'll be at the next rehearsal. When does it meet?"

"Every Saturday morning at nine, in a rehearsal room at UCLA. But you have to have your own instrument. It's not like a marching band, where you can check one out."

He looked at the sky. "Lord, Lord, when will they learn? Sybil, or whatever your name is, I will be there Saturday morning, and I will bring my own instrument. And though my tubaphone is big, my car is bigger, thus leaving enough space for one tiny passenger such as yourself. Would you care to ride with me to the rehearsal?"

Now it just so happens that getting to and from rehearsals had always been a problem for me. Being seventeen, I'd had my driver's license for over a year, but a car never seemed to be available. So for a while I'd gone on the bus, which took the best part of an hour, and more recently I'd taken up the Brodys on their offer to let me ride with them in their Bentley. Sitting in the same car with Mr. Brody was bad enough. But when you added to that the queen of the social-ites, Mrs. Brody, and their daughter Mitzi, who played at the flute and reminded me of a pink-ribboned poodle—the kind that wags its tail and then throws up on your carpet—the combination was too much. Week by week, as they drove me to rehearsals, they had also been driving me slowly insane. Now the question became, would I rather go crazy little by little with the Brodys, or all in a blazing flash with this new duck-footed, knock-kneed, acne-scarred threat to my mental health?

"Okay, I'll go," I said.

So maybe I was already crazy.

4

"What is this stuff, anyway?" I asked.

My dad leaned over my plate and carefully spooned a pale yellow mixture onto the food before me. He did the same to the food on his own plate, then took off his chef's hat and apron and hung them on a peg next to the stove. Seating himself across from me, he sampled the mixture, licking his lips in the same dainty way he always did when tasting fine food. "Mm, perfect," he murmured, his eyes glazed.

"Dad, remember me?"

He looked up. "Huh?"

"Hello, Mars."

"Oh, sorry, Sizzle. What were you saying?"

"I was saying, what is this stuff?"

"Eggs Benedict. It's an English muffin with Canadian

bacon and a poached egg, topped off with hollandaise sauce."

" 'Topped off with'? You're beginning to sound like those cookbooks you're always reading." It was true. He read cookbooks the way most people read magazines. He kept a big stack of them by the john, and more than once I had surprised him in bed with Julia Child.

"Check it out," he said. "It's good, Sizzle, no kidding."

I dipped my fork into the concoction and tried a bite. "Really terrific." I took another bite and smiled at him. "Your best yet."

"You think so? Gee, thanks." His face lit up as bright as a brand-new frying pan, and beneath his shaggy mustache I could see a broad grin.

The truth was, my taste in food ran more to quantity than quality. I couldn't tell the difference between eggs Benedict and an Egg McMuffin, between ragout and ribs, between vichyssoise and vegetable soup, but I would never admit that to my dad. Aside from jazz and baseball, cooking was his life. Well, he also delivered mail, but that didn't count. It was just a way to keep a roof over our heads and trout meunière on the table.

Saturday was his day off, and he always celebrated by whipping up a gourmet breakfast for the two of us before I headed off to rehearsal. We had had Belgian waffles, eggs rancheros, soufflés, croissants, and omelets of every size, shape, and description. I would have been just as happy with bacon and eggs, but not my dad; and that was the important thing.

I looked across the table at him, where he sat, lost in his eggs Benedict. He was a tall, wiry man who from a distance looked younger than his thirty-six years. I guess what did it was his boyish face and the long hair tied in a ponytail.

When you got up close, though, you could see a network of wrinkles around the corners of his eyes and mouth, and suddenly he looked old. He had never looked like that before the divorce.

He and my mom had met on a picket line in Berkeley, where between demonstrations they were going to college. They were student activists—in those days I guess they were called hippies—and when they fell in love, neither realized that the main thing they had in common was their opposition to the Vietnam War. In their sophomore year they were married, an act which to their friends seemed more radical than any sit-in, and a year later I came along.

My dad tells me it was tough after they got out of college and the war ended. They had answers for the world's problems but none for their own. Such as 1) What do you do with two bachelor's degrees in English literature? 2) How do you make a real home for yourself and your family? And 3) What's the next move when you wake up one morning and realize you no longer love the person you're living with?

It took them ten years to find the answers. In my dad's case, the answers were 1) become a mailman, 2) hang out, and 3) make the best of it. Unfortunately, his answers didn't mesh too well with my mom's, which were 1) become a lawyer, 2) get organized, and 3) get a divorce. When things settled down, she was at a law firm in New York, dictating letters to everybody but us. And he and I were eating *coq au vin* in Mar Vista, perhaps the only community in Los Angeles where you can live near the beach and still cash a check without three credit references, a Mercedes pink slip, and a note from your stockbroker. It was also one of the few places in L.A. that had anything resembling decent bus service—a necessity since my dad's car, an ancient Hillman named Ché Guevara, was in constant need of repair.

I finished my last bite of breakfast and pushed back my chair. "Got to get going, Dad. My ride'll be here in a minute." I leaned across the table and kissed him on the cheek.

"Say hello to the Rockefellers for me," he said.

"Dad, it's the Brodys. And I'm not going with them today. I got a ride with someone else." Outside, a horn sounded. "Uh-oh, that must be him."

He grinned. "Him? You got a ride with a boy? I don't believe it."

"Dad, it's called transportation."

"That's his name?"

"No, his name is—never mind, it's a long story." I hurried across the room, picked up my trumpet case, and headed for the door. Lounging against it was my dad's basset hound, Mellow. Actually, Mellow wasn't so much a pet as a piece of furniture. He spent so much time lying around that we had considered putting coasters under his elbows. I took hold of his collar and pulled him across the carpet and out of the way. He never even opened his eyes.

"See you later, Dad," I called.

It was as fat as a hippo and as heavy as a Sherman tank. It had wide whitewall tires and a front end that would accommodate place settings for twelve. If a car could get pregnant, this is what it would look like.

Sitting proudly behind the wheel was Arthur Hadley Reavis Pauling the Third. "It's a 1949 Packard Custom Eight," he said, "and if you so much as smudge it, I'll beat you to within an inch of your overdrive."

"I knew you were strange," I said as I climbed in, "but this goes beyond my weirdest expectations."

"Thank you."

"That wasn't a compliment."

"You take what you can get."

With a low rumble that might have been the purring of a giant cat, the car pulled out into traffic. As we drove down Sepulveda Boulevard, Splat gave me a tour of his Packard. "Note the distinctive pearwood graining on the dashboard and door panels. That's real wood, folks, not plastic. The seat backs are filled with duck down, and the seat frames are decorated with leather. The floor is covered with luxurious cut pile carpets." He gestured toward the ceiling. "And please don't overlook the distinctive woolen headlining with fore-to-aft seams."

"Where did you get this thing?"

"From an old lady down the street named Mrs. Goldfarb. She was the original owner and had driven it to the grocery store once a week for over thirty years. In all that time, the only change she'd made was to add seat belts. I used to wax the car for her, and when she decided to sell it, she offered it to me first."

"I guess a car like this wouldn't cost much, huh?"

"Are you kidding?" he bleated. "I could get ten thousand dollars for it tomorrow."

I checked him for diamond jewelry and Gucci loafers. All I saw were jeans and a T-shirt that read *A day without Pachelbel is like a day without sunshine.*

"Of course," he added, "I didn't pay that much for it. Mrs. Goldfarb was more interested in finding a good home for her car than in making money, so she let me have it for five hundred and a written promise to take it to Palm Springs once a year."

Up ahead I saw a welcome sight. "Can you pull into this McDonald's?"

"Didn't you have any breakfast?"

"Yeah, but I'm hungry again."

Five minutes later we were heading down Sepulveda Boulevard once more and I held in my lap a Big Mac, fries, and a shake. "For crying out loud, be careful with that stuff," Splat said. "Spill fries on the seat and you'll be eating your trumpet for dessert."

He turned a knob on the dashboard, and suddenly we were in Symphony Hall. "The stereo's my only concession to modern technology in the whole car. And in case you didn't recognize it, that's Bruckner's Fourth Symphony, with Otto Klemperer and the New Philharmonia Orchestra." Keeping one hand on the steering wheel, he picked up my straw with the other and began conducting.

"I'll watch the fries if you watch the road," I said.

"So what's the story on this Pirelli Youth Orchestra?" he asked a few bars later.

"It's like most youth orchestras, only better. There are kids from junior high to college in it. We do four concerts a year, and Mr. Pirelli has us play all the best symphonic music. He says he's trying to start us off with good habits while we're still young. That is, I think it's what he says. He's kind of hard to understand."

"What do you mean?"

"Well, he talks fast. But the main problem is he seems to have no native language."

"Isn't he Italian?"

I gulped down the last of the malt. "Not exactly. See, his father was Italian, and his mother was Hungarian. He'd been dragged all over Europe by the time he was five, picking up inflections the way most people collect souvenirs. The man's a walking United Nations. He's inarticulate in sixteen languages."

"Yeah? Tell me more."

"There's no more to tell. I only know that much because

of a story he told us in rehearsal. Every once in a while he mentions something about his past, but not often. He doesn't like to talk about himself. He says he'd rather talk about music."

"I like him already." Using my straw, Splat cued the trombones.

"If you're interested in the orchestra, there's something else you should know. It's in financial trouble. We're giving a benefit concert to raise money, and if that's not a big success, it's good-bye Franz Schubert, hello Forest Lawn."

"Forest Lawn—student of Beethoven, right?"

"It's a mortuary, wise guy. But before you start humming the Verdi Requiem, listen to this: Hans Kleiman's writing a special piece for the concert. It'll be a world premiere." I didn't mention the fact that it was going to be a trumpet concerto because—you guessed it—I don't like to toot my own horn.

Splat gave a low whistle. "Hans Kleiman, huh? How'd you manage that?"

"His nephew, Buckminster Brody, is president of our orchestra association, and up until recently was our biggest contributor."

Splat turned up the volume on his stereo. "This last section is great!" he shouted over the din, and began waving the straw around like some kind of crazed musketeer. He cued the cellos, poking me in the side of the head.

I moved away. "Would-be conductor held in brutal straw slaying—film at eleven."

He glared straight ahead, still beating furiously. "French horns! Brass! Tutti, tutti!" As the last chord sounded, he gripped the straw until his knuckles turned white, his arm quivering like that of a fisherman fighting a shark. Then he took a deep breath and with all his remaining strength drove the arm down and across his body in one final, convulsive sweep. The chord echoed through the giant bathtub of a car, then died away. Splat was left panting, clutching in his hand the crumpled remnants of his red-and-white-striped baton. "I think I just saw God," he said.

"You did?"

Splat nodded. "He looks a lot like Bruckner."

5

"Ladies and gentlemen, we begin please at letter *P*. This is coming into the last movement."

Vidor Pirelli moved nervously about the podium, flipping through the pages of the score, pulling his earlobe, smoothing his hairpiece, seizing on any small motion to pass the time, which moved so much more slowly than he did. With his long nose and jerky movements, he always reminded me of a bird. Sometimes when he conducted I half expected him to leave the ground and circle the orchestra, chirping rapid-fire directions to each section as he passed overhead.

I opened the first trumpet part of the Sibelius Second Symphony and turned to letter *P*, one of many key points in the music marked with a letter for rehearsal purposes. As I did, I glanced down the row of brass players to where Splat was sitting, his instrument nestled in its case several feet away. Pirelli, afraid that two tubas playing at once might overpower the rest of the orchestra, had asked him to alternate with the regular tuba player, Eddie Greenbaum. Since Eddie was playing the first half of the rehearsal, Splat was resting. Actually, what he was doing was picking his nose.

Pirelli tapped his baton on the podium. "Before we begin to start," he said at his usual auctioneer's pace, "we must know the meaning behind our music. Mr. Jean Sibelius wanted freedom for his Finland peoples, and in this Second Symphony he shows them the way. At letter *P* we can hear the peoples calling for freedom, and then rumblings of excitement grow as they see it far away. It gets close and close, and then at letter *R* freedom is here; it is so happy. Now come on."

He turned to his left, where the sleek Anthony Formica and his band of ragtag followers sat. "Young people of the violins," Pirelli said, "your beautiful notes here are the rocks on which your colleagues in woodwinds and brasses build. Please to rehearse it now."

"Mr. Pirelli," came a voice from the back of the section, "he's pulling my hair!"

"She started it! She stuck her gum on my violin."

"That's not my gum. That's been there for a month!"

It wasn't exactly the New York Philharmonic. Pirelli was well aware of that, but he still viewed these outbursts with alarm. "Please, Jerry and Sandra, please! Do you pull hairs in church? Do you chew your gums in the synagogue? Act right. We are in the cathedral of music. Mr. Jean Sibelius is trying to speak to us." Jerry and Sandra glanced warily at each other, then turned back to their music.

Pirelli had the violins play their part, reminding them of bowing techniques and warning them not to slow down in the difficult passages. Next he combined the violins with the violas, cellos, and basses. Satisfied with the strings, he turned to the woodwind section.

"My young friends the woodwinds, your turn now comes. While the violins sing out their hearts in a steady beat, you run along with shouts of excitement. 'Look!' you are saying. 'Look, it is coming, it is coming! Freedom, isn't it lovely!' All right, letter *P*, we now try it."

He gave them the downbeat, and there it was, just as he said. You could hear the excitement and see it in the woodwinds' faces. Pirelli might talk funny, but the guy knew how to rehearse. And that, no matter what people might tell you, is what makes a good conductor. Never mind all the dancing and flailing and pirouetting that some of these guys insist on. If a conductor does his job in rehearsal, all he really has to do in the concert hall is beat time.

Finally Pirelli looked up at the brass section. "You are so lucky, you peoples, because Mr. Jean Sibelius has given the greatest honor to you in this symphony. You are freedom itself, shining bright and so pretty over the orchestra. Please now to play your part, and let us all listen to freedom."

It was the kind of passage brass players love, the kind that keeps you going when you're sitting there counting rests, wondering why the violins get all the fun parts. We must have done a good job playing it, because when we stopped there was a moment of silence before Pirelli murmured, "Ah, yes, my young friends.

"And now," he went on, "we ask our colleagues in the percussion to join in, and we put all the sections together at the same time. Come on now—letter *P.*"

The music began. The strings swirled and throbbed, then came the cries of the woodwinds, and finally, soaring above it all, the brass. As we launched into the fanfare at the

27

beginning of the last movement, the feeling started. It was a dizzy sort of feeling, a floating sensation as if suddenly I was way up in the sky looking down. It was a feeling of rightness, of everything being just as it should be, and along with it there was a tingling like an electrical current. Maybe this was what Pirelli meant when he talked about the cathedral of music. On the other hand, maybe I was just hyperventilating.

"All right, peoples," Pirelli said when we had finished rehearsing the Sibelius, "please now turn to *Pictures at an Exhibition,* by Mr. Moussorgsky. As you play, pretend you be strolling very nice through a museum, with many paintings hanging on the walls. As you stop and look at each one, you sing out how it make you feel. Some are happy, some are depress, some are angry— Listen close to the music and you see what I mean. We begin, please, at letter *T.* This picture is an old man pushing his cart steady down the old cobbled street. We have a tuba solo, which we shall play on baritone horn. Carl, please to get your instrument."

The baritone horn is similar to the trombone in range and tone, so it is usually played by one of the trombonists. But as Carl Freidlander, the first trombonist, reached for his baritone, a voice came from the end of the row. "Why don't we play it on the tuba?" It was Splat. "We can do it, can't we?" he asked Eddie Greenbaum. Eddie, who was apparently familiar with the solo, shook his head. "Well, then, I'll give it a try," said Splat. He rose from his chair and went over to take his tuba out of its case.

"You are Arthur, isn't this true?" asked Pirelli. They had met briefly before the rehearsal.

"That's right."

"Well, Arthur, I must thank you extremely, but this solo plays too high for the tuba."

"Not for my tuba." He lifted the instrument and hefted it over to his chair, where he sat and rested it in front of him. The tuba was a gleaming Mirafone, a German model with rotary valves and an upright bell. Seeing it with Splat was like seeing a Mercedes parked in front of a Quonset hut. "Ready when you are, maestro," he said.

Pirelli smiled uncertainly and raised his baton. "Ladies and gentlemens, please, letter *T*."

With the downbeat, the string basses began a mournful tune, and Splat started in. I cringed as he attacked his first note, because I was sure it would prove that his nickname had more to do with tubas than toads. To my amazement, the tone that came out of that bell was full and round and golden. Heads turned and eyebrows rose as the solo went on. It was a sad melody, somehow resigned and dignified at the same time. As Splat played it, you could imagine every aching muscle on the stoop-shouldered old man in the painting. I guess you might say Splat was doing what Pirelli constantly asked us to do in our music: Tell a story.

When the last phrase died away, Pirelli made a motion I'd never seen him make before. He laid down his baton and started applauding, and everyone else joined in. "Bravo, young tuba friend," he called. "Bravo, Arthur." The only one who wasn't clapping was Eddie Greenbaum, and you couldn't blame him. It's pretty hard to congratulate somebody for taking your job away.

In the second half of the rehearsal, the brass section sounded better than I'd ever heard it. With Splat playing tuba, our chords were fuller and richer because we had a strong foundation to build on. The guy was so good that he made you forget what he looked like and how he acted. Well, almost.

At noon Pirelli stopped us. "That's finish for today, ladies and gentlemens. You play lovely for me this morning. Keep that safe in your heart for next week, and we will do this again." As he closed his score, one of the parents hurried up to the podium and handed him a note. Pirelli read it silently, his swarthy face turning several shades lighter.

"Young friends," he said after a moment, "I have a sad news. Mr. Kleiman went to hospital last night. He died from cancer this morning."

6

Sometimes when I'm practicing my trumpet, one of the notes causes something nearby to hum. The humming is sympathetic vibration, and it means that at that moment my trumpet and the object are pulsing at the same rate. Maybe the object is a smudged glass. Maybe it's a paper clip or a three-ring binder. It may not remotely resemble my shiny silver-plated trumpet, but the humming proves that they're alike in some mysterious way.

That's how it was between Hans Kleiman and me, even though we'd met only once. Next to him I was just a smudged glass, but when he spoke I could feel his words, almost like I was saying them. I'm not mentioning this to brag but to explain how I felt when I heard he was dead. It was like somewhere deep inside me there had been a melody, and now it was silent.

On the way back from the rehearsal, Splat had the good sense not to talk. When I got home I found my dad lounging in front of the TV. He was staring at the screen, absently scratching Mellow, who lay next to him like a discarded throw rug. "Have a seat, Sizzle," he said. "You're missing a good cooking demonstration."

I walked past him and headed for my room. "No, thanks."

I was lying on my bed when he came to the door. "You okay?" I nodded. He studied my face for a minute, then walked over and sat down next to me. He pushed the hair out of my eyes and touched my cheek, and I guess that's what finally did it. I could feel my chin start trembling and my throat getting tight. I tried to stop it by thinking of something else, like the wallpaper pattern or chromatic scales, but it was too late. Tears were spilling out of my eyes onto his hand.

"Remember Mr. Kleiman, the man I told you about?" I said. "He had cancer. He died this morning." I put my arms around my dad's middle and held on tight.

He squeezed back, his strong hands gripping my shoulders. "I'm sorry, Sizzle, I really am."

"I feel like I did when Grandpa died. Like a door slammed, and he's on the other side."

"I know what you mean."

I rubbed my cheek against his soft flannel shirt, then I pulled away and wiped my eyes with my hand. "I didn't mean to get carried away."

"Sizzle, why are you always trying to act so tough?"

"I guess I just don't like to cry."

"Crying's not so bad, you know. It's just a way of feeling something sad—or something beautiful."

"Do you love me, Dad?"

"I sure do."

I hugged him and grinned into his shirt. "More than Caesar salad?"

"Well, it's hard to beat a good Caesar salad. Let's just say you're both right up there."

"Promise you won't leave me?"

"I promise."

"Promise you'll do whatever you can to make me happy?"

"Um-hm."

"Then could you make me a couple tuna fish sandwiches? I'm starved."

I followed him into the kitchen, and there on the table was the mail. At the top of the stack was a manila envelope with my name and address printed in large block letters. Puzzled, I opened it up and pulled out the contents. It was the trumpet part for Hans Kleiman's concerto.

I sank into a chair and shuffled through the music. Clipped to the back were a typed page, a sheet of nonsense words, and a handwritten letter. I looked at the letter.

Dear Sizzle,

I'm dying. I don't usually like to be so blunt, but I can't afford to waste what little time or energy I have left. I would have called and asked you to come visit me, but I've been trying to finish the piece. I composed during all my waking hours, and even so I've just barely been able to complete it. I thought of you often while I worked; so although I haven't seen you, I feel as if we've been in touch.

This is my finest piece, Sizzle. In it I've been able to interweave my two great loves, music and games. The music is a message to the world, telling people how I feel about living. (Isn't it odd that in dying one learns so much about living?) Like life itself, the music has hidden meanings and surprises. The game is also a message, in the form of a cryptogram. I don't think I'm boasting unnecessarily when I say that this cryptogram will guarantee the success of the Pirelli Youth Orchestra's benefit concert. In fact, I would suggest renting a bigger hall.

Sizzle, you play a very important part in this piece —quite literally. Meeting you inspired me to write it, and now I'm depending on you to present it to the world. Knowing you, I'm sure you'll do that in fine style.

The details of the music and the game will be given to the press by my attorney, Marcel Lombard. But since you are so important to the entire project, I'm enclosing advance copies of the trumpet part, the game, and the program notes, which I wrote myself. To avoid any misunderstanding, I must ask you to keep these advance copies a secret. No one knows of them but you and me.

Please don't feel sad about my dying. Remember the rose, and think of this music as my last blush of color. We met only once, Sizzle, but when you play my concerto, we will meet again.

Your friend,
Hans Kleiman

My dad says crying is a way of feeling something sad or beautiful. I'd already cried for something sad. I like to think that my new tears were for something beautiful.

After lunch I went back to my room and looked over the

rest of the materials. I tried playing the trumpet part but couldn't tell much; without the orchestra accompaniment, it was like listening to one end of a phone conversation. So I went on to the program notes.

Trumpet Concerto in G Major

If music is good, it needs no explanation; if it is bad, no amount of explaining can help. So rather than presenting detailed program notes, I will simply state that this concerto has three movements: the first, an *andante*; the second, a *rondo*; and the third, another *andante*, then *allegro con brio*. All three are woven around a recurring theme, which is the key to the music:

The Game

A cryptogram, or coded message, will be handed out to ticket holders at the beginning of intermission. Before the concert resumes, ushers will collect answers, and during the playing of the trumpet concerto these will be checked. At the end of the concert, the winner will be announced. The prize is five hundred dollars, which I am donating.

Non-ticket holders, including orchestra members, are ineligible for the five-hundred-dollar prize. If more than one person correctly decodes the message, a drawing will be held to select the winner.

Hans Kleiman

Kleiman knew perfectly well that the five-hundred-dollar prize would make our benefit concert the hottest ticket in town. If his concerto by itself guaranteed a sold-out auditorium, then the concerto and game together might give us a shot at filling the Sports Arena. In one last stroke of genius, Hans Kleiman had saved the Pirelli Youth Orchestra.

I set aside the program notes and looked at the sheet of paper beneath it. On it was Kleiman's final game—the cryptogram itself.

HLLG KLR RL WLPIQ, UTR RL JTQES;

ERQ JYQRCPECQ MPC ICCNCP,

ERQ PCWMPIQ AMP BPCMRCP.

Staring at the jumbled letters, I couldn't help but wonder if Kleiman hadn't made a terrible mistake. Did he really think someone could make sense of this mess during a twenty-minute intermission?

I fiddled with the code for an hour or so and, not having much experience with cryptograms, got nowhere. I made a quick copy of it on a scrap of paper and slipped it into my wallet, figuring I could take it to the library sometime and try again, with the help of a book on codes. Of course I wasn't eligible for the prize, but it might be fun to solve the cryptogram on my own.

That done, I picked up my trumpet, put the solo part on my music stand, and spent the rest of the afternoon in the company of my friend Hans Kleiman.

7

![checkered pattern]

"Here it is," I said. " 'Composer Leaves Unexpected Gift for Youth Orchestra.' Part 5, page one of the *L.A. Times.*"

It was the following Saturday morning, and because of Mr. Brody's pain at the loss of his uncle, I had done something I'd vowed I would never do again: ride to rehearsal with Arthur Hadley Reavis Pauling the Third. But that day, not even Splat could bother me, because I'd gotten a call from Pirelli saying he'd received a package in the mail containing the game, the program notes, and a complete set of orchestral parts. We'd be rehearsing the concerto that morning.

"So what are you waiting for?" said Splat. "Let's hear the article."

"Temper, temper." I raised the newspaper and began to

read. " 'Well-known composer Hans Kleiman, who died last Saturday of cancer, had just completed a new concerto shortly before his death. Commissioned by the Pirelli Youth Orchestra, the concerto will be premiered next month as part of a fund-raising concert. But now, according to Kleiman's attorney Marcel Lombard, the orchestra will be receiving a bonus. It seems that Kleiman, an avid game player, devised a game to go with the music and donated five hundred dollars to be used as a prize for the winner. Since only those attending the concert will be eligible for the prize, it is anticipated that ticket sales will skyrocket, providing the Pirelli Youth Orchestra with an unexpected financial boost. Tickets will go on sale in two weeks.' "

"Wow," said Splat. "What kind of game do you think it is?"

I almost mentioned the cryptogram but then remembered Kleiman's request for secrecy. "I don't know. But Mr. Pirelli should have more information on it this morning."

"What about the concerto? I can't wait to play it." A dreamy look crossed Splat's cratered countenance. "Maybe it's for tubaphone. I've always felt there was a shortage of tubaphone concertos."

"There's also a shortage of square bowling balls."

"I won't dignify that with a response."

"Face it, Splat. Asking a tuba to play a concerto is like asking a hippo to dance *Swan Lake*. Besides, I already know what the piece is. It's a trumpet concerto."

"What? He passed up the tubaphone for that glorified piece of tinfoil you play?"

"Flattery will get you nowhere."

"And I suppose you're going to be the soloist?"

"Let's just say the part calls for a five-foot eleven-inch female of Polish extraction."

"Lord, I believe she's serious."

"It's a great piece—you'll love it."

"How do you know?"

"Just a hunch."

Ten minutes later we were in the hallway of the music building at UCLA. We heard an excited buzzing up ahead and saw a crowd of people clustered around the door to the rehearsal room.

Splat eyed the group. "Probably one of those Veg-O-Matic demonstrations."

I hurried forward and shouldered my way through the crowd. When I peered into the rehearsal room, I couldn't help but gasp.

Chairs were overturned. Stands were bent into grotesque shapes. Music was strewn from one end of the room to the other. Light fixtures were shattered, and broken glass covered everything.

But worse than all the damage was the note that had been scrawled on the blackboard: Do not play the Kleiman Trumpet Concerto.

"Why in God's green apples would anybody do such a thing?" demanded Vidor Pirelli. "Can any of you here tell me that?" As he looked at each of us his jaw moved up and down like a high-speed engine revving before a big race.

Pirelli, Brody, Formica, and I were holding an emergency meeting of the orchestra steering committee in the one corner of the room left untouched. The rehearsal had been canceled, and we had spent the last hour talking with Detective Niles Denton, a chain-smoking police officer wearing a wrinkled trench coat and fedora. Now Denton, with Splat's unsolicited help, was moving about the room, combing the mess for clues and taking notes on a small pad.

Nearby, Mitzi Brody flitted around taking pictures of the scene with a small plastic camera.

"Just as I told Detective Denton," Anthony said, "the reason is obvious. Someone didn't like Hans Kleiman."

"But he was such a nice, that is, gentle sort of man," said Mr. Brody.

"It seems to me," I suggested, "that this isn't the time or place to figure out who did it. The important thing is, what are we going to do about it? Should we go ahead and play the piece or not?"

Pirelli slammed his fist into his palm. "Yes, of course so. The Pirelli Youth Orchestra shall not be stop by a common hoodling."

Anthony brushed some lint from his slacks. "I agree with your sentiments, Mr. Pirelli. But we don't know how far the hoodlum is willing to go. What if he tried to hurt someone?"

"Hurt someone?" asked Brody, suddenly concerned. "My goodness, I hadn't thought, it hadn't occurred to me that there might be physical danger involved. You don't think the person, that is, the vandal would stoop to such tactics, do you?"

"That's just the point," Anthony said. "We don't know. Are we willing to take that chance?"

"I am," I said. "Are you?"

Anthony cleared his throat. "Of course, I'm the most visible member of the orchestra, so I have more reason to be concerned."

"I suppose the rest of us sit behind bulletproof shields," I said.

"Bullets?" croaked Mr. Brody.

"There shall be no bullet in the cathedral of music," said Pirelli. "There shall be simply music, wrote by our belated Hans Kleiman."

"I don't know, Vidor," said Brody, his eyebrows wiggling furiously. "We're entrusted with, that is, responsible for the lives of eighty young people. The most important thing is to make sure they're safe, don't you think?"

"Music, not bullet," Pirelli answered, crossing his arms.

"Look," I said, "we don't have to decide anything right now. Why don't we wait and see what the police find out? There's more than a month before the concert, and we can prepare another piece just in case we have to drop the Kleiman concerto."

"This makes good sense, Prudence," said Pirelli. "We can wait to see."

"I still don't like it," commented Anthony.

"It makes me, that is, my initial feeling, the way I look at it . . ." Buckminster Brody stopped and sighed. "I'm scared."

8

Splat leaned back against the distinctive pearwood graining inside the door of his 1949 bathtub and popped a fried onion ring into his mouth. "The police aren't going to investigate, you know."

I had asked Splat to pull up to a fast-food stand on the way home from the canceled rehearsal. Mysteries make me hungry. But then, so do badminton matches, algebra exams, garage sales, and anything else short of stomach surgery.

"Of course they'll investigate," I said, biting into my second cheeseburger. "They've got to—a crime was committed."

"Nope. I was talking to Denton, that detective. He said the police are understaffed and have to spend their time on important things, like murders."

"But this is important, too. Kleiman's concerto might be canceled. . . . Somebody might even get hurt."

"You and I know it's important, but Denton doesn't. Which is too bad, because he's got one very good lead. The custodian was cleaning another room early this morning and heard a noise. When he looked out the window, he saw a green Buick driving out of the parking lot."

"That's a good lead?"

"Hey, it was four thirty in the morning. There was nobody else around. But is Denton going to follow it up? No, he's too busy." Splat jabbed the air with an onion ring. "You know, there's something we can do about this."

"Such as?"

"Investigate it ourselves."

"By 'ourselves,' do you mean myself and yourself?"

"That's right."

"Forget it," I said.

"But think of all we've been through together—the hamburgers, the fries, the tacos. . . ."

"I guess I'm just not sentimental."

"Then think of the orchestra. Think of Hans Kleiman."

I pictured Kleiman's Santa Claus face smiling at me and realized Splat had a point. At that moment, I made my decision. "You're right. I'll investigate this thing after all."

"Great!"

"By myself."

"What? How can you say that?"

"It's all in the vocal cords."

"But you need me to work on the case with you," he insisted.

"Give me one good reason."

"I have a mind like a steel trap."

"I'm pretty hardheaded myself."

"I have a complete set of Agatha Christie mysteries."

"I don't like to read."

"I have a funny, crooked grin."

"Crooked, maybe."

"I have a car."

It was true. He did have a car. And suddenly, I had a headache.

"I'm glad you see it my way," he said. He tilted his head and gazed off into the distance. "You know, Sizzle, a mystery is like a symphony. It has a single theme unifying it from beginning to end, and the alert observer, by noting the development of that theme, can often name the composer— in this case, our culprit. Stop me if this is going over your head."

"Nothing's going over my head, but this malt may be going over yours."

"There are many possible themes to a mystery," he went on. "Jealousy, for example, is always nice. Revenge can be fun. Sheer unadulterated hatred is effective if handled with a light touch. Then there's my personal favorite, passion."

"Look, this is serious. Vandalism's nothing to joke about."

"Who's joking? I'm just laying a little philosophical groundwork for the case."

"So that's what the shovel's for."

"All right, all right, maybe it's too early to pick out a theme. But we can start by answering one very important question: Who stands to gain if the Kleiman concerto is canceled?"

"Nobody does. That's what makes the whole thing so crazy."

Splat held up one greasy finger. "Ah, yes, but someone must, otherwise there would have been no crime. It seems to me there are two groups who stand to gain: enemies of Kleiman and enemies of the Pirelli Youth Orchestra."

"What enemies? We're talking about a kindly old man and a bunch of underage musicians."

"Don't worry, everybody has enemies. Our job is to find out who they are."

"And how do we do that, smart guy?"

"The first thing is to get an information source, somebody who's familiar with both the orchestra and Kleiman."

"Buckminster Brody."

"Perfect! I tell you, we're going to be one of the all-time great teams—bigger than Laurel and Hardy, Astaire and Rogers, Gilbert and Sullivan, Dorfman and Dern. . . ."

"Who are Dorfman and Dern?"

"See? We're bigger than them already."

Monday after school we went to visit Brody, whose company was located in a gleaming high-rise building on Wilshire Boulevard. The office itself took up the entire twentieth floor. A woman in a shapeless polyester dress sat at the reception desk just inside the door reading a paperback novel.

"Can I help you with something?" she asked, glancing with distaste at Splat's faded jeans and T-shirt, which said *Bach in the saddle again*.

"We're Prudence Szyznowski and Arthur Pauling," I explained. "We have an appointment with Mr. Brody."

Splat looked down at the cover of her book. "*My Secret Lust*," he read. "I've heard that's good."

The woman stuffed the book into a desk drawer and consulted the calendar in front of her. "Yes, here we are. Just a moment, please." She picked up the phone and pressed a button. "Mr. Brody? Miss Semanski and Mr. Pollette are here to see you."

45

"Tell them they'll have to wait," Splat said. "We got here first."

The woman took great care to avoid looking at Splat. "Mr. Brody will see you now," she said to me. "He's in the fourth office on the right."

As we walked down the hall, I noticed that the place wasn't exactly humming. In fact, two of the three offices we passed were empty. In the third was a man who either was daydreaming or had quietly passed away several days before.

The fourth office had an open door bearing the nameplate BUCKMINSTER BRODY, PRESIDENT AND CHAIRMAN OF THE BOARD. Inside, fiddling with a paper clip, sat the great man himself.

"Hello, Prudence," he said, rising to greet us. "And it's Arthur, isn't it?"

Splat shook Brody's hand. "Pauling's my name, tuba-phone's my game."

The office had a plush, overstuffed look, as if the decorator had tried to crowd as much as possible into it, hoping to impress visitors with sheer quantity of gewgaw. The furniture was elegant, though worn.

"Mr. Brody," I said, "I've always wondered—what business is it you're in?"

"Property, that is, real estate. And various other investments." It fit in with what I had always heard—that Brody's money was inherited and his business consisted of managing that inheritance.

We started to sit down, but Brody stopped us. "I usually get a snack about this time every afternoon. I wonder if you'd join me."

"I will," said Splat, "but Prudence probably wouldn't be interested."

"It's okay," I said. "I'll force myself to eat something."

46

"Is Perino's all right?" Mr. Brody asked. "It's just a few steps, that is, a short walk down the block."

"Whatever," I replied. As he led us out of his office, I shot a glance at Splat, who looked back with raised eyebrows. Perino's was one of the most expensive restaurants in Los Angeles. Going there for a snack was like using gold bullion for a paperweight.

As we walked down Wilshire, among the business people and afternoon shoppers, Splat told Brody we'd been wondering if either the orchestra or Hans Kleiman had any enemies he knew of.

"Not enemies," he said. "Certain rivals, perhaps."

"Such as?"

"Well, there's William Cranston. He's the conductor of the Los Angeles Youth Symphony, and I'm sure he'd like to see his orchestra overtake and pass ours. But he wouldn't resort, uh, stoop to vandalism and threats."

"How about Kleiman's rivals?" said Splat.

"I believe there were some composers who were jealous of his success. Aunt Frieda would know more about them."

"Would it be okay if we talked to her?" I asked. "It hasn't been long since her husband died, and we wouldn't want to upset her."

Brody considered the matter for a moment. "I don't think she'd mind. I just—"

An arm encircled Brody's neck, and his eyes bulged open wide. A gloved hand brought the butt of a revolver down with a sharp crack on the top of his head, and Brody slumped backward. Before we'd had time to think, Buckminster Brody was being dragged into a waiting car by a burly man wearing an overcoat, a tennis hat, and a mask.

Like virtually everyone else on the sidewalk, I stood frozen by the suddenness of the violence. Only Splat moved to respond. With a quickness that surprised me, he launched his scrawny frame at the man's upper body. As he tried to pull Brody free, the butt of the gun came down again, this time in the vicinity of Splat's eye. He stumbled back, then rushed forward again, but the car door had already slammed.

By then I had recovered enough from my shock to try and help out. I ran toward the car, and as Splat tugged the handle of the front door, I tried to open the back. Both were locked. We pounded on the windows, but now all we could do was watch. The man in the overcoat jammed the car into gear and shot out into traffic. Before he disappeared around the corner I had just enough time to notice that the car was a small brown Toyota sedan, late seventies model, with dents on the back and side. The license plate was covered.

The whole thing had taken no more than fifteen seconds.

I stood there, stunned. A crowd was gathering, craning their necks to see what had happened.

"Will you stop gawking and call the police?" I yelled at them. Then I remembered that the man had hit Splat, and I looked over at him. There was a nasty cut just below his left eye, and blood was dripping down his cheek.

"Does it hurt?" I asked.

"I guess we miss out on Perino's," he said.

Twenty minutes later, Detective Denton was there with a team of investigators, talking to witnesses and looking for clues. Immaculately rumpled, Denton was obviously a great admirer of old detective movies. The coffee-stained trench coat, the fedora pushed back on his head, the brown wing tip shoes, the cigarette dangling at the corner of his mouth —all the details were just right, except for one: He had the face of a choirboy. I put his age at twenty-five.

He circulated through the crowd, barking questions at onlookers and getting descriptions of the kidnapper as being everything from a renegade butler to a five-hundred-pound orangutan. By the time Denton got around to us he was understandably skeptical, even though Splat claimed to have a good nose for detail.

"Brute Force!" Splat exclaimed.

"Look, kid," said Denton wearily, stamping out a cigarette butt, "dwelling on that bump you got isn't going to—"

"No, Brute Force, the men's cologne. That's what the guy had on. And besides the cologne, he was wearing a cheap wig."

"What, was there a price tag on it?"

"Look, Mr. Denton," I said, "in case you didn't notice, someone's been kidnapped. We're just trying to help."

"I know someone's been kidnapped!" he growled, flipping through his notepad. "But with this kind of information I'll never catch the guy who did it. You know what I got here? Zip. Zilch. Nothing."

"I think this might be related to the vandalism with the Pirelli Youth Orchestra," Splat said.

"Are you serious?"

"Sure. Brody's president of the orchestra association. There's got to be a connection."

"Brody's also president of the Buckminster Brody Corporation," Denton said. "He drives a fancy car and lives in a mansion. Translation: money. Believe me, fella, this kidnapper's more interested in that than in a bunch of punk kids sawing away on dime-store violins. It's a ransom case—I guarantee it."

That evening, Mrs. Brody phoned me to say that an unidentified caller had informed her that her husband would be returned unharmed after the Pirelli Youth Orchestra's benefit concert, provided the orchestra did not play the Kleiman Trumpet Concerto.

9

■□■□■□■□

"Oh, my aching head," moaned Vidor Pirelli. "I never want to view again one single reporter and camera. Flash! Flash! Talking! Talking! These peoples don't ever get tires."

Splat and I were sitting with the conductor in his office. It had been two days since Buckminster Brody had been kidnapped, and the press coverage was just beginning to die down. Mr. Pirelli wasn't the only one who had been kept busy; Splat and I had been pestered by reporters and even had our pictures in the paper. Splat's cut had turned out to be no more than a glorified scratch, but it gave him a black eye that the caption called a battle wound. He'd been disappointed to learn from his doctor that the swelling would go down inside a week.

"Mr. Pirelli," I asked, "what are you going to do about the Kleiman concerto?"

"There aren't any choice. In my palms I carry the life of my friend Mr. Buckminster Brody." He shook his head sadly. "There shall be no Kleiman music for our concert. I have lock all of it away. The hoodlings have won."

Hans Kleiman had said in his letter he was depending on me to present his music to the world. Now it seemed I wouldn't be playing it at all—unless the man in the overcoat, whom we'd started calling Mr. X, was captured and brought to justice before the concert.

"Maestro Pirelli—I can't tell you how shocked I am." We turned to see who had spoken, and there in the doorway stood a three-hundred-pound tomato.

"Mr. Cranston, please to come in," said Pirelli. "Prudence, Arthur, this is Mr. William Cranston, most proud conductor of the Los Angeles Youth Symphony. Mr. Cranston, these young peoples make some of my fine brass section."

This was the first time I'd actually seen Cranston. What surprised me wasn't so much his size—that I'd heard about —but rather his age. He couldn't have been more than twenty-one. His skin was smooth and unlined. He had pale blond, neatly combed hair and what could only be called baby blue eyes. As if to counteract these features, his brow, cheekbones, nose, and chin jutted forward defiantly and on a thin man might even have been called angular. He wore a red sweater, red slacks, and white patent leather shoes that resembled twin yachts.

He heaved his way into the room, his face flushed and his sides almost touching the doorframe. We shook hands. It was like squeezing a jellyfish.

"Sit, please to sit," said Mr. Pirelli.

"Yeah," said Splat, "pull up a chair. Pull up several chairs."

Cranston shot Splat a tight smile. "Thank you, no. I can only stay a minute. I just wanted to say how concerned I am about Mr. Brody. And I wanted to see if, under the circumstances, you were going ahead with the Kleiman piece."

"No, by all means no," said Pirelli. "We cannot put our Mr. Brody in some danger."

Cranston sighed, and his features relaxed. "What a shame. It would have been a wonderful fund raiser."

"You look pretty broken up about it," I said.

"Prudence!" said Pirelli.

"It's all right, maestro," said Cranston. "She's just upset. When dealing with children as often as I do, one learns to take these outbursts in stride."

I would have said something else, but I didn't want to make Mr. Pirelli mad. Besides, I was afraid Cranston might sit on me.

"Well," said the huge conductor, "I'd best be going. My orchestra is doing *Ein Heldenleben* in a few weeks, and I need to study the score. If you're a brass player," he said to me, "you should come hear us. You might find it instructive. The concert will be Thursday night, October—"

"I'll look for it in the paper."

"Yes," he replied, "of course. Well, it was a pleasure meeting you. And maestro, please let me know if there's anything I can do to help. I hope your Mr. Brody will be all right. But then, I'm sure he will be."

"Thank you, Mr. Cranston," said Pirelli.

With that, William Cranston turned around and guided his immense bulk out the door.

Pirelli eyed me sternly. "Prudence, you must learn some of manners."

"I'm sorry. I guess he just bothers me."

"Don't you be silly now. William Cranston is nice young man."

"Yeah," I said quietly. "He's swell."

"That's the word for him, all right," said Splat. "Swell."

10

▪▫▪▫▪▫▪

We had made arrangements to visit Mrs. Brody the following Sunday to see if we could turn up some new leads. But when the day arrived, Splat's car was in the shop getting a tune-up. Since we didn't want to cancel our appointment, I coaxed my dad into letting me borrow Ché Guevara, which was getting a rare visit home from its usual location at Ollie's Organic Auto Repair.

I picked up Splat and we headed for the Brodys' house, a medieval castle located between a Georgian mansion and a Mayan temple on a quiet residential street in Beverly Hills.

When we knocked on the heavy wooden door, Mrs. Brody answered. Her hair, usually immaculately coiffed, was done up in a rude bun. There were bags under her eyes, and she was wearing the plainest of cotton shifts. If she had shown up at one of her famous cocktail parties looking like that, she would have been hustled out the back door.

"Hello, Prudence," she said, her voice and her shoulders sagging. "Come on in, both of you."

We followed her through a high arched entryway into what she probably referred to as a sitting room. I would have called it a den. We sat down on an L-shaped sofa that looked like it could use reupholstering.

"Are you thirsty?" Mrs. Brody asked. "My help is off today, but I suppose I could get you something to drink." Her remark had all the enthusiasm of an offer to change the oil in my car.

"That's okay," I said. "We'll only be a second. It was nice of you to let us come over."

"I haven't been talking to many people," she admitted, "but you're a little different, since you were there when it happened." She looked at Splat and winced as she studied the black-and-blue marks around his eye. "You're Arthur, aren't you? I'd like to thank you for trying to save my husband. How's the swelling?"

He shook his head sadly. "Not too good. Doc says it won't last more than a few days."

"We just have a couple of questions, Mrs. Brody. I hope it doesn't bother you to talk about this."

"I don't mind. But shouldn't you leave it to the police?"

"We're doing some checking on our own," I said. "It won't interfere with what the police are doing." I took out my notebook and a pencil. "After your husband was kidnapped, you got a phone call. What did the person tell you?"

"I can't remember his exact words; I was too frightened. But basically he said Buckminster was perfectly all right and would stay that way as long as the orchestra didn't play Uncle Hans's new piece."

55

"Do you remember what the man sounded like?" asked Splat. "Could you recognize his voice if you heard it again?"

"I'm afraid not. The sound was muffled, like he was holding something over the receiver. And he was speaking very slowly."

"The guy was disguising his voice," I said, taking a few notes. "Just like he disguised his appearance."

"Mrs. Brody," said Splat, "could anyone have known the exact time your husband was going to leave for a snack?"

"I suppose the people in his office. And the staff at Perino's. He goes there every afternoon at the same time. That's my Buckminster. He's a very meticulous man."

We asked her a few more questions and turned up nothing. As we were about to leave, Mitzi got home. After nodding uncomfortably to us, she kissed her mother and held up a green envelope. "I got my pictures back," she said.

"That's fine, dear. We'll look at them later."

"Wait a second," I said. "You were taking pictures the day the rehearsal room was vandalized, weren't you?"

"Yeah, they're right here." She handed me the envelope. With Splat peering over my shoulder, I shuffled through the snapshots until I came to what I wanted. There were six pictures of the damage, and looking at them I felt the same sickly jolt I had felt that day. The only difference was that now the jolt was more intense, because the damage reminded me of the violence Buckminster Brody had suffered a few days later.

Mrs. Brody apparently had the same reaction. "Can we put those away?"

I was about to hand them back when I noticed something. The last two pictures showed people crowded in the doorway, gawking at the destruction. Among the onlookers was a man who by his sheer bulk would dominate any scene. The man was William Cranston.

Splat saw it too and gave a low whistle. "What would Cranston have been doing there?"

"Scouting the competition, maybe," I said. It was obvious from Splat's expression that he didn't believe it. Neither did I. "Mrs. Brody, these last two pictures are almost identical. Would you mind if we kept one? You'll still have the negative if you need it, and we'll return the print as soon as we can."

"I don't see any harm in that." She took the pictures back, all except for the one, which I slipped into my pocket.

"If Cranston's our man," said Splat when we got back into Ché Guevara, "then he must have hired Mr. X to do his dirty work for him."

"Makes sense."

"What doesn't make sense is the motive. Rivalry between two youth orchestras? You don't kidnap somebody over that."

"Don't be too sure."

"Maybe there's something about Kleiman we don't know. We could— Hey, wait a second! There's a green Buick parked across the street."

"I hate to tell you, but the kidnapper was driving a brown Toyota."

"Would you kidnap somebody using your own car? The Toyota was a rental. This could still be him."

"Splat, how many green Buicks do you figure there are in Los Angeles?"

"Look, he's slouched down in the seat, trying to hide."

"Is there some law against pulling over and catching a quick nap?"

"In Beverly Hills, yes. Besides, he's not asleep. I'm going to talk to him."

Splat got out of the car and started across the street toward the Buick. As he did, the man covered his face and reached for the ignition. The engine roared to life, the tires squealed, and the Buick shot forward.

Splat whirled and got back into the car. "We've got to chase him!" he yelled, bracing himself with one skinny arm on the dashboard.

"You've been watching too many movies."

"Follow that Buick!" he shouted, his one good eye glistening with excitement. I could tell it was no use arguing.

I turned the key. Ché Guevara backfired once, then lurched out of the driveway and into the street. The Buick was in sight long enough for us to see it squeal around the corner onto Cañon Drive, heading for Sunset Boulevard. We followed, going as fast as the car would allow.

"I want to see what he looks like!" screamed Splat. "Pull up alongside him!"

I yelled back, "The only thing this car pulls up alongside is stop signs."

The Buick sped across Sunset Boulevard and onto Benedict Canyon Drive. As we reached the intersection several seconds later, the light turned yellow. I leaned on the horn, downshifted, and just made it through before the light changed.

"We're in the canyon now," said Splat. "We should be able to use our cornering ability to catch up."

We went around the first curve at forty, and the car tilted so badly Splat had to hold on to keep from sliding across the seat.

"When's the last time you had the shocks replaced?" he demanded.

"Right after the Civil War. No, come to think of it that was just an oil change and lube."

I had to slow down to take the next corner, and by the time we rounded it there was no sign of the green Buick. We tried a few side streets, but it was no use.

"We had him," moaned Splat, "and he slipped away. We didn't even get close enough to see the license plate. If only we'd had my Packard. We would have caught him easy. Easy."

"You know," I said as we headed down a side street, back toward Benedict Canyon, "this neighborhood looks familiar. I've been here before, but I can't remember who I was visiting."

I didn't remember until later that day. I'd been in Benedict Canyon several months earlier, for a meeting of the orchestra steering committee. The meeting had been held at Anthony Formica's house.

11

The Frieda Kleiman who sat across from us was very different from the woman I had met a month before. Her smile was gone, and the lines in her face had deepened.

"I never got a chance to say how sorry I am about your husband," I said. "If I'd known he was sick, I would have come by to visit."

"Hans spoke about you so often, I feel as if you *did* visit. Please don't feel bad." In the cavernous drawing room, Mrs. Kleiman seemed tiny, defenseless, lonely. "His death was difficult, but I'd been expecting it because he'd had cancer for years. What I didn't expect was this kidnapping. Buckminster is such a dear man—why would anyone do it?" Her voice grew hoarse and trailed off. "I can't understand such things."

"We just want to ask you a couple of questions," I said. "We won't keep you long."

"When we spoke to Mr. Brody," said Splat, "he told us that some of the other composers at UCLA were jealous of the attention your husband got. Who—"

"I'm sorry," she said abruptly. "I really don't want to talk about that."

Surprised, Splat looked over at me. It appeared the interview would be even shorter than we had expected.

I pulled Mitzi Brody's snapshot out of my pocket and handed it to Mrs. Kleiman. "Of the people standing in the doorway, do you see anyone you know?"

She glanced at the picture, then handed it back to me. "No, I don't."

Her eyes told me differently.

"She's scared," I said. "Somebody's told her not to talk about her husband."

We were sitting in Westwood's tackiest Chinese restaurant, where I had ordered my favorite—the MSG combination plate. As for the interview with Frieda Kleiman, it had been cut short a few minutes after I produced the picture.

"It wasn't so much her husband she didn't want to talk about," said Splat. "It was his music she wouldn't discuss—and the jealous composers at UCLA."

I took the snapshot out of my pocket and looked at it. "Do you think she recognized Cranston?"

He shook his head. "How would she even know him? When would they have met? No, I have another idea."

Fifteen minutes later we entered the UCLA music building. It was familiar to both of us as the place where the Pirelli Youth Orchestra rehearsed. Splat led the way up the stairs to the main office of the music department, where just outside the door was a large bulletin board with the name and office number of each faculty member. Next to each name was a photo.

"Splat, you're brilliant," I said.

He smoothed his hair. "And you thought I was just another pretty face."

"Brilliant but strange."

I held the snapshot up to the bulletin board and ran it down the column of photos.

In the faculty photo he was dressed in a coat and tie. In our snapshot, standing in the doorway, he was wearing slacks and a sweater. But it was unquestionably the same person. He was a broad-shouldered, athletic-looking man in his fifties, with short hair and finely chiseled features.

" 'Dr. Lane Weatherby, Department of Composition,' " read Splat.

"At your service," said a voice behind us.

I stuffed the snapshot into my pocket and turned around. Facing us was the man in the picture. He was smiling, but his eyes were ice cold. "May I help you with something?"

"We, uh, were just hoping to talk with you," I said. "We wanted some information about Hans Kleiman and were told you were a friend of his."

"You were told wrong. Hans Kleiman and I didn't like each other. It was no secret."

"Could we talk to you anyway?" asked Splat.

"I have a class in a half hour. I can give you a few minutes, but I warn you, I don't have anything pleasant to say about Kleiman."

His office, like his grooming, was immaculate. There were a number of framed documents on the walls, including several foundation awards for composition. "You've gotten a lot of recognition," I said.

He smiled bitterly. "From the foundations and critics, yes. From the public, no. They save their applause for Hans Kleiman and his ilk."

How can you trust someone who says *ilk* with a straight face? "You may not have liked Kleiman," I said, "but you have to admit he was a pretty good composer."

"No, I don't. He composed for the masses, trying to appeal to them with catchy melodies. He always left the audience with a tune they could hum on their way out of the auditorium."

"Got something against humming?" asked Splat.

Weatherby eyed him the way you might look at a spider in your bathtub. "Truly modern music cannot be hummed."

"How about whistled?"

The composer took a deep breath and let it out. Judging from the size of his chest, he either did a lot of weight lifting or worked weekends moving furniture. "Let me explain something to you. Modern composers have two choices: They can copy music of the past or create music of the future. Those of us serious about our work have chosen the latter path."

"Yeah," said Splat, "I've heard some of that music. Sounds like a computer mating with a garbage truck."

Weatherby looked straight at him for several seconds. "I think you'd better go. I have to get ready for my class."

"Dr. Weatherby," I said, "why were you standing in the doorway of the rehearsal room the morning it was vandalized?"

"Young lady, are you accusing me of something?"

"Just asking a simple question."

"And I'm giving a simple answer: Get out of my office, and don't come back."

We started to leave, but Splat paused in the doorway. "Just one more thing. Do you drive a green Buick?"

"I drive a jet black Mercedes. If I owned anything even resembling a green Buick, I would destroy it with a sledge-hammer."

"Put it on tape and you've got your next symphony," said Splat as we exited.

Outside, Splat turned to me. "Did you notice?"

"Notice what?"

"He was wearing a wig."

12

■□■□■□■□■

"Pauling!" yelled Miss Kelly. "How many times do I have to tell you—step off on your left foot!"

"Which one?" asked Splat.

She covered her eyes with her hand.

The marching band was practicing formations on the football field. In the process, Miss Kelly was discovering what I had learned weeks ago: Splat was . . . well, different.

Most people are embarrassed by their shortcomings; Splat flaunted his. He had scrawny arms and a concave chest, so he wore T-shirts that were a size too small. When people stared at his duck-foot walk, he would look at them and quack. His most alarming feature was his complexion, and yet aside from music it was his favorite topic. He even wrote a paper about it for health and family life class and called it

My Acne, My Friend. The paper categorized zits by type, including the cyclops, the volcano, and the many-chambered nautilus.

Splat believed, in short, that the best defense was a good offense. He cultivated his handicaps and used them as weapons, like an invalid beating someone over the head with a crutch. It hadn't occurred to me until recently that no one goes to such lengths to defend himself unless he's afraid of being hurt.

"Pauling," Miss Kelly was saying, "you're a valuable part of my game plan. You're the bottom line of this band. But you've got to straighten up and fly right or all of us will be left out in the cold."

"I'll give 110 percent," he promised.

"That's music to my ears, Pauling." She turned to the rest of us. "That wraps it up for today. We'll give it another whirl tomorrow, but with instruments. Dismissed—all except Pauling."

She had apparently decided to hold Splat to the extra 10 percent he had promised, because for the next half hour she drilled him on his marching techniques, which for Splat consisted of column left, column right, about face, and fall down. By the time they finished, the sky was getting dark and I was getting impatient for my ride home.

After exchanging parting clichés with Miss Kelly, Splat and I walked to his car. Without thinking, I tried the handle on the passenger side, and the massive door swung open.

"Hey," said Splat, "I locked that."

"Everybody slips up once in a while."

"With my Packard I never slip up." He walked around and examined the door, then let out a cry of alarm. "The wind wing—it's broken!" He bent over it like a parent over

66

a dying child. Then he inspected the rest of the car. There was no other damage.

"They must have wanted something inside," I said. "I wonder—my trumpet! It was on the front seat!" In place of the missing trumpet was a piece of paper. I saw that it was a note, written in the same scrawled hand as the message in the rehearsal room:

" 'You'll find your trumpet under the east goalposts on the football field.' Wait a minute—we were just out there."

"And we're going back," said Splat, relocking the car door.

As we hurried to the field, I kept thinking about my trumpet. It was a silver-plated, large bore Bach that had taken me a year to save for. I'd ridden the bus all the way over to a music store in Glendale, a trip of two hours, and had tried out every trumpet in the store. When I got to the last one, as soon as I blew the first note, I knew it was something special. It's hard to believe that a bunch of plumbing can have a personality, but this plumbing did. It had nobility, style, class. I named it Wellington.

The football field was dark when we got there, but we could make out the east goalposts standing like sentries in the moonlight. Under the goalposts was a black shape. I raced over to it, and Splat followed.

I bent over and examined the case. It looked fine. I took a deep breath, popped the spring-loaded catches, and opened it.

"Oh my God," said Splat.

Wellington had met the enemy and lost. Its tubing was twisted, its slides and crooks were bent at grotesque angles, and its glorious silver bell was crumpled up like a wad of paper.

There was another note attached. It said, "Stop investigating, or you'll end up looking like this."

That was when we heard the gunshots.

Splat grabbed me, I grabbed Wellington, and the three of us ran. We dove behind a nearby wall and peeked out to see where the shots were coming from. There was a flash of orange, and another shot rang out.

"Up on the hill, in the trees!" I whispered. "I'm going to sneak around behind him."

Now, before you conjure up Saturday-matinee images of the good guy circling around behind the bad guy and jumping him, let me tell you two things. One, I am not now, nor have I ever been, a member of the Roy Rogers fan club. Two, what am I, nuts?

The fact is, I would never have tried such a stunt if I hadn't known something the gunman didn't know—namely, that the wall led to a pedestrian tunnel which in turn led to a bus stop about twenty yards behind where he was standing. Once I reached the bus stop, I had no intention of trying to catch the guy. All I wanted to do was cower in the tunnel and see what he looked like.

As soon as the next shot rang out, I took off along the wall. I ducked into the tunnel, where I sprinted through broken glass and up a long flight of concrete steps. When I neared the top I realized the shots had stopped. I had a vision of the gunman crouched in the shadows just outside, and my confidence seeped away like air from an inflated toy. Trying to keep from panting, I stepped forward and peered out. No one was waiting in ambush. Encouraged, I took another step and looked toward the trees where the shots had been coming from.

There was a sudden crunching sound, and a figure burst out from among the trees, running full speed. I ducked back into the tunnel, but I soon realized he wasn't coming in my direction. I poked my head out again and tried to make out what the man looked like. I didn't see much, because by then he was a good fifty yards away, with his back to me. But I saw enough of the broad-shouldered silhouette to convince me it was the same man who had kidnapped Buckminster Brody. The car cinched it—a green Buick. He jumped in, slammed the door, and raced off down the street. Once again I was too far away to read the license plate.

When I rejoined Splat on the field, he gave me a brief, vivid lecture on personal safety, and then I told him what I had seen. While he was digesting the new information, I went over to gather up Wellington. I was just about to latch the case when I remembered.

"Splat, there was something in my case. It's gone."

"What was it?"

I wasn't supposed to tell anyone, but then I wasn't supposed to get shot at, either. "The Kleiman Trumpet Concerto and the game that goes with it."

"*What?* Why didn't you tell me before?"

I latched the case and started toward the car. "Come on, let's go to my house. We need to talk."

69

13

There's nothing like a few gunshots to get the old digestive juices flowing. When we got home, I heated up some frozen pizza and a few cans of chili—Dad would have objected, but he was out for the evening—and Splat and I sat down to eat and talk. I mentioned the letter from Hans Kleiman and its warning not to discuss my advance copies. "I'm only telling you now," I said, "because of everything that's happened. I think Mr. Kleiman would have understood."

"Did anyone know you kept the music and game in your trumpet case?"

"No one even knew I had it, let alone where I kept it."

"So we can assume Mr. X was surprised when he found

it there. And what did he do? He took it. Doesn't that tell us something?"

"Maybe he wanted to see it for himself."

"Or," said Splat, "he didn't want you to study it any more than you already had. Either way, he's given us a clue."

"Get to the point, Sherlock."

"We've been so busy trying to sniff out Kleiman's and the orchestra's enemies that we've overlooked the most obvious piece of evidence in the whole case: the game. Maybe that's where we'll find the answer to this thing. But," he said, suddenly looking tired, "now it's gone."

I pulled a crumpled sheet of paper out of my wallet. "I made a copy so I could work on it at school."

"That's great!" He took the sheet from me and looked it over. "Hey, a cryptogram. I'm good at these."

"Splat, there's something else. I think we need to go to the police."

"We already talked to them. Denton's a moron."

"Listen, genius, those were real bullets. That was a real gun. And I'm getting real scared."

"Does this mean you want to drop the case?"

I nodded. "I think we should tell Denton everything we know and let him handle it. Splat, we're in over our heads. Instead of saving Mr. Brody, we're liable to put him in more danger, or end up kidnapped ourselves."

"But we're just about to crack the case."

"The only thing that'll get cracked is our skulls. I'm going to Denton."

"You trumpet players are real wimps, you know that?" He shook his head in disgust. "Okay, so we go to Denton. But first let's solve the cryptogram to see if it gives us any new leads. Denton's going to need all the help he can get."

We pushed our empty dishes aside and concentrated on the message. "This looks like what's called a substitution code," he said. "Each letter equals another letter—simple."

"Great."

"Or not simple."

"Not great."

"It depends on the particular code."

"Not particularly great."

"Besides my awesome deductive powers," he said, "we've got one big factor going for us—Kleiman designed the code to be broken in twenty minutes. So I figure it shouldn't take us more than, say, two years, tops."

"In that case, let's get started."

"Ever tickle an ostrich?"

"Beg pardon?"

"No, I'd rather suck hummingbirds."

"I'll leave now."

"What you've just heard, Sizzle, is a mnemonic device."

"Sounds like something a plumber would use."

"He might, if he happened to be absentminded. A mnemonic device is a trick to help you remember something—in this case, the most commonly used letters in English, in order of frequency. Ever tickle an ostrich? No, I'd rather suck hummingbirds—E, T, A, O, N, I, R, S, H."

"Let me guess—you made up those sentences yourself."

"That's amazing. How did you know?"

He jotted the letters down on a sheet of paper and below them wrote the entire alphabet, spaced neatly. Then together we charted the number of times each letter appeared in Kleiman's message. For the next hour or so we used that chart and Splat's mnemonic device to make educated guesses as to what the letters in the message stood for. When that didn't work, we fiddled around with various substitution patterns, based on frequently used letter combinations and short words. When that failed, I put on a few records and we fiddled some more, hoping Strauss, Copland, and Bartok might give us a clue. Miraculously, they did.

"Music," Splat murmured, and began writing feverishly on a blank sheet of paper.

"Very good," I said. "And we call those flat round things records."

"No, music. The word *music.*" Five minutes later he showed me his work. On the sheet of paper, he had once again written the letters A through Z, and above the first five letters he had put M U S I C, followed by all the remaining letters of the alphabet. "It's called a key-word code. The records reminded me to try what had to be Kleiman's favorite word, and *viola*—our answer!"

"You mean *voilà.*"

"Hey, we're talking music here."

At the bottom of the page was Hans Kleiman's message.

LOOK NOT TO WORDS, BUT TO MUSIC;

ITS MYSTERIES ARE DEEPER,

ITS REWARDS FAR GREATER.

"Too bad we're not eligible for the five hundred dollars," said Splat. "I guess Mrs. Kleiman gets it back."

"Yeah, but Splat, you solved it! That's terrific!"

He gazed at the page. "But what does the answer mean?"

"Well, I can think of two things. Number one, Kleiman was a philosopher."

"And number two?"

"Time to go see Denton."

The office of Detective Niles Denton was impeccably seedy. In the midst of a well-furnished Los Angeles police station, he had somehow latched onto a gray metal desk, a broken-down chair, and a dented wastebasket. He had removed the standard-issue round light fixture overhead, leaving just a bare 60-watt bulb that cast a dingy yellow beam around the room. In front of him on the desk were piles of memos, an ashtray full of cigarette butts, and a worn paperback copy of Raymond Chandler's *Farewell, My Lovely*.

"What'll it be, Szyznowski?" he asked, his cigarette bobbing.

"We've got more information about the Brody case. We were doing a little investigating of our own."

He frowned. " 'A little investigating'? That's like a little knowledge—it can be dangerous."

"Yeah, well, that's part of the information. We sort of got shot at." We told him about the trumpet, the note, and the ambush, and he made out an incident report. Then we worked our way back through everything that had happened since the kidnapping. We told him about Mitzi Brody's photo. We described the chase through the streets of Beverly Hills. We showed him the decoded message. And we filled him in on the evidence regarding our two chief suspects, Cranston and Weatherby. Splat and I took turns speaking, supporting and embellishing each other's remarks like soloists in a double concerto. There was no denying it —our findings were impressive.

"I'm not impressed," said Denton. "The only thing you've shown me is you're lucky you weren't hurt. Your so-called evidence is a joke."

"But you've got to admit," said Splat, "Cranston and Weatherby have been acting suspicious."

"Okay then, what's their motive?" He leaned back and sent two smoke rings swirling toward the ceiling.

"Ambition for Cranston," I replied. "Revenge for Weatherby."

Denton chuckled. "Ambition in a kiddie orchestra? Revenge against a dead man? Get serious."

"If we're so far off the mark," I said, "why did Mr. X wreck my trumpet and leave that note, then shoot at us?"

"He left the note because you know what his car looks like and he doesn't want you chasing him any more. He shot at you because he's stupid."

"Maybe he only decided to shoot at us after he found the music and game in Sizzle's trumpet case," Splat said.

Denton shook his head. "The game was a cute gimmick and no more."

The guy was starting to get on my nerves. "Okay, then who did it?"

He squinted at me through the smoke for several seconds. It was a pose I'd seen Bogart strike a hundred times. "Well, obviously the concerto is central to this whole thing, but that doesn't mean this 'Mr. X' is a musician. Matter of fact, most kidnappings involve one of two things: politics or money. It's easy to see which category this one fits. That's the angle we've been following up."

" 'We'?"

"The FBI's working with me on the case. They help out on all kidnappings."

"What have you found?" asked Splat.

"I'm not at liberty to divulge that. All I can say is, we've been talking to Brody's business associates—his employees, his clients, people like that. I guarantee you we'll have more luck with our angle than you've had with yours."

"Have you traced the Buick?"

"We put it into our computer and got a list of over a thousand green Buicks in West L.A. alone." He took one last drag of his cigarette and snuffed it out in the ashtray. "Now get out of here, and leave the investigation to us. I'd hate to see a couple of dandy kids like you get hurt."

As we were walking out the door, Splat turned back to Denton. "Aren't you even going to talk to Cranston and Weatherby?"

"Yeah. If I ever want advice buying classical records."

14

■□■□■□■□■

"Ladies and gentlemens, there is some several things you may care to know about Mr. Richard Wagner. One thing is the saying of his name—Reekard Vahgner, that is how you say it. If you say it in the American way, he sound like a smiling man on TV. And may I tell you, young friends, he most certain was not that. For the number two thing about Mr. Wagner is, simply and truly, he was a very bad person. He never pay his bills. He not kind to his friends. And with the ladies, he love and leave them."

Vidor Pirelli paused and surveyed the rehearsal room. Gradually he began to smile. "Ah, but his music, his music. In some way, a great love shine through his music, and this I cannot ever understand. But I am surely grateful, and believe you me, all of you will feel this, too. For today we play the wonderful overture to *Die Meistersinger*. Please, take it from your folders and we now may discover the terrible and wonderful Mr. Richard Wagner."

No matter what was happening in the rest of my life, I could always count on Mr. Pirelli and symphony rehearsal to make me feel good. I'd been depressed ever since Splat and I had gone to Denton the week before, but as the orchestra played the overture, I felt my spirits rise. Considering I was playing on a borrowed trumpet, it was a pretty good trick.

"Brass," cried Pirelli over the music, "if you please, louder and more full. When you playing, the gates of heaven must open!" I doubled my efforts, and the music soared, taking me with it.

When the last chord died away, Pirelli kept his eyes closed for a full five seconds. "Yes," he murmured. "Yes, my young friends."

He looked at his watch. "There is no more time for today. But before you are leaving, there is something I must tell." He set down his baton and smoothed his hairpiece, then cleared his throat before starting. "Ladies and gentlemens, you know that our benefit concert will be in just three short weeks from now. Of course we shall not play the Mr. Hans Kleiman concerto because to keep safe our dear Buckminster Brody. I know we all praying for him every single day, so he must be let go safe and soundly when our concert is finish. But I must tell you this: Our money is lacking just the same, and now that we don't play Mr. Kleiman's music, we probably won't getting the big audience we want. Which mean, I am sorry to say, our lovely orchestra will not go on very much long. It seem that this most likely can be our last season. I want to just play and play, sharing music of Mr. Wagner and Mr. Beethoven and Mr. Ravel with all of you so eager. But after this season we cannot. Without money, our hands must be tied together. This is sad, but this is truth." He closed his music, picked up the baton, and stepped off the podium.

Somewhere in the back of my mind I had known this moment was coming, but with Kleiman's death and Brody's kidnapping there had been other things to think about. Now there was no avoiding the realization that the Pirelli Youth Orchestra's days were numbered. I packed up my trumpet and walked slowly over to where Splat was sitting. He was wearing a *Handel with care* T-shirt.

"Great news, huh?" I muttered.

"Wait a second or two, then turn and look out into the hallway. Try not to be too obvious about it."

"What are you—"

"Just do it."

I took a step back and, as casually as I could, glanced over my shoulder toward the hall. There I saw Anthony Formica in conversation with someone whose face was familiar and whose massive body was even more so. It was William Cranston.

I stepped back toward Splat, who was hurriedly putting his tuba into its case. "Don't forget," he said, "when we chased the Buick into the canyon, we ended up near Formica's house." His voice grew tense. "They're leaving together."

"Maybe we should call Denton."

"I've got a better idea—let's follow them ourselves." He got to his feet and picked up the tuba case.

"Hey, the investigation's over, remember?"

"Funny, I'm drawing a blank on that." He started toward the door.

I followed. "Let me refresh your memory: mangled trumpet, threatening note, gunshots, bullets, possible trouble, possible death. . . ."

"We're going to lose them. Hurry up."

I hesitated in the doorway. My practical side was telling me to turn around and go back into the room. But then, I hadn't been listening much to my practical side that morning. Another part of me had been playing Wagner and listening to Pirelli's announcement, and now it was that same part that propelled me through the doorway and into the hall.

"They're headed toward the parking lot," said Splat. Bracing the heavy tuba case against his right side, he lurched down the hall like a man with a broken leg.

The car they got into wasn't the green Buick; it was a late model Porsche, though how Cranston could afford it on a conductor's budget was as big a mystery as how he could fit inside. We piled into the Packard and followed them down Gayley to Westwood Village, adjacent to the UCLA campus. They found a parking place on Westwood Boulevard, an occurrence about as frequent as appearances of Halley's Comet.

As they got out of their car, Splat moaned, "We're going to lose them. We've got to park somewhere, fast." He swung over into the left lane, spun the wheel, and made a U turn before a phalanx of oncoming traffic.

"Hey, take it easy," I said, hanging on to the armrest.

"Up ahead on the right, look!" He pointed to a Volvo about to back into a parking place. "Hang on!" he cried, leaning over the wheel like a fighter pilot over his controls.

"We can't take this space—it belongs to the Volvo. I hate people who do this."

Quite obviously, so did the man in the Volvo. A few seconds later, when he realized his space was gone, he got out of his car and came back to discuss the subject. His basic point was that Splat would look good with a terse message carved into his forehead.

Dodging traffic, we sprinted across Westwood Boulevard just in time to see Cranston and Formica taking a table at a sidewalk café. "We've got to hear what they're saying," Splat said.

I glanced around, looking for possibilities. "Follow me."

I led the way through a clothing shop next door and out the back entrance into an alley. From there we entered the kitchen of the sidewalk café, where we were greeted with hostile stares.

"Health inspectors," I said. "Sponge off those pork chops." We hurried to the indoor dining area and from there surveyed the outdoor tables. Cranston and Formica were seated nearest the sidewalk with their backs to us. Next to them was an empty table.

"May I help you?" said an oily voice just behind us. We turned to see the host eyeing us warily, his fingers drumming the stack of menus he was holding.

"We were supposed to meet some friends here," I said.

"There they are now," said Splat. He grabbed my hand and pulled me through the front door out onto the patio. I kept waiting for Cranston and Formica to look up and see us, but they were engrossed in their menus. We took seats at the adjacent table.

"Please, Anthony, this is my treat," Cranston was saying. "Order whatever dish strikes your fancy." The man oozed charm. Come to think of it he oozed, period.

"What do you suggest?"

"Everything's delicious. I've eaten it all." Indeed.

"I'm starting to feel guilty," Formica said after a few minutes. "It's like I'm betraying the orchestra."

"Don't be absurd. You're just thinking of your own career. Now that the Kleiman concerto won't be played, the Pirelli Youth Orchestra is dead. You'd be foolish not to switch over to my group."

"I guess you're right," Anthony mumbled.

"Of course I'm right. We'll be paying you three times what Pirelli pays, for one thing." Formica was one of perhaps ten key members of our orchestra who were in the musicians' union and received payment for their work. "But the big thing is your solo work. I'm guaranteeing you three concertos a season. If our plan works out, Pirelli's orchestra will fold and mine will take its place as the best-known youth orchestra in the country—a perfect launching pad for your career."

It was one thing to speculate about Cranston and Formica's scheme; it was another to hear them actually discussing it. For a moment I felt sick.

"What'll it be?" It was our waitress.

"Water's fine," I said in a low voice.

"You'll have to order more than that, honey," she replied.

"Water with a twist," Splat said.

"Listen, we got a three-dollar minimum per person. So what do you want?"

"We want you to leave," said Splat under his breath.

"I heard that," she said. "And I think the manager would like to hear it, too." She stomped off.

"Time to go," I whispered.

Splat threw his arms around me and plastered his lips to mine. I made a frantic effort to push him away, but he whispered in my ear, "Cranston's looking at us. Try to hide."

I nuzzled his neck and felt him bury his face in my hair. After a moment, I adjusted slightly and peeked with one eye toward Cranston. He had turned back toward Formica.

"The coast is clear, Romeo," I said.

"Now," boomed a voice from nearby, "what seems to be the problem here?"

I pushed my way past the manager, dragging Splat behind. "No problem," I said. "No problem at all." We ducked back inside to retrace our steps. As we zigzagged among the tables, I looked over my shoulder.

"Actually," I murmured, "there is one problem."

Cranston and Formica were staring right at us.

15

"Great, Splat, really great."

"Hey, I was just trying to do a little detective work. So there were a few minor slipups."

"Slipups? First you steal a parking space, then you get smart with the waitress, then you use me to practice your mouth-to-mouth resuscitation. And by the way, I took a first-aid course, and mouth-to-mouth does not involve the tongue."

After leaving the restaurant, we had called Denton to tell him what we'd found. He wasn't in, so we left a message and headed home. All the excitement had made me hungry, so on the way back to Mar Vista we had stopped at the Santa Monica Mall for a quick fix of junk food. I was trying to drown my worries in preservatives; but as I poured more salt over the french fries, I knew it wouldn't work.

"They warned us to stop investigating, and we didn't," I said. "It wasn't just your fault; it was mine, too. I went along. Now they might come after us. Or they might take it out on Mr. Brody—that'd be ten times worse. I feel terrible."

"But we got a break in the case."

"That may not be the only break we get. Remember what they did to my trumpet?"

"You've got to stop thinking like that, Sizzle. Come on, let's do something to take our minds off it."

"Like what?"

"There's always mouth-to-mouth resuscitation."

"Over my dead body."

"Hey, kinky."

"Did I ever tell you you're totally disgusting?"

"You may have mentioned it."

"I'm mentioning it again."

"Don't mention it."

"How did I ever get mixed up with you?"

"First I was mixed up. Then you were mixed up. Now we're mixed up together. There's nothing confusing about it."

"Sorry I asked."

"Sizzle," he said, and suddenly his face was serious. "There's something I have to tell you. It's been building up inside of me, and I just can't hold it back any longer."

Oh, God. "Splat, do we have to talk about this now?"

"Yes, we do. Otherwise I'll think of it every time I look at you. And I don't know if I could stand that."

He was a nice guy, really. In the last few weeks I'd grown

85

to like him, in spite of his strange looks and sense of humor —maybe even because of them. I took a deep breath. "All right. What is it?"

"You've got chocolate malt on the end of your nose."

After we left the fast-food place, we went walking in the mall—or rather, I walked and Splat did an awkward sidestep waddle alongside, trying to convince me he deserved to live. So far I wasn't buying his arguments.

"I've got it," he said. "I know just the thing to make you feel better: Tchaikovsky's *Romeo and Juliet*—music to soothe the savage breast."

"You mean beast."

"That too. Come on, here's the record store."

Arnie's Music wasn't your usual sort of record store. The thing that made it different was a row of listening booths in which prospective customers could sit and preview albums they were thinking of buying. Whatever income Arnie lost in making demonstration albums available was more than made up in increased traffic, because the booths faced the mall's main corridor and were glassed in from floor to ceiling. Watching people in the brightly lit booths was almost as popular as playing video games in the arcade.

Usually, sitting in a booth at Arnie's was fun. If you got bored with the music, you could act out little scenes for the people outside. You could pretend to cry or laugh or fall asleep with your mouth open. But today I was nervous. I knew it was probably my imagination, but I kept seeing glimpses of a man in an overcoat.

"Splat, I think someone's watching us," I said over the opening section of *Romeo and Juliet*.

"Of course someone's watching us. You can see the people right through the glass."

"Not that kind of watching. I mean *watching*."

"You're right," he said, suddenly developing a facial tic. "Have to give them a good show."

"I'm not kidding. I think Mr. X might be out there."

"Hey, listen to this," Splat said. "The good part's coming up." He leaned toward me. "Listen to those strings. Listen to those French horns. Speaking of French . . ."

I edged away from him. "What's the matter with you today?"

"Nothing. Nothing at all." He turned to the window for a moment, then lunged toward me. I felt his arms tighten around me and his body press against mine.

"Splat!"

There was a crashing noise, and suddenly the booth was filled with shards of flying glass.

When I opened my eyes, I was sprawled in the chair with Splat lying dazed on top of me. Beyond him was a large metal trash bin, one corner of which was jutting through what used to be the glass wall of our listening booth.

A woman was standing over us, screaming. Behind her, a crowd had gathered.

"Splat," I said, "are you all right?"

"Huh?"

The screaming was like an air raid siren, only louder. "Hey," I yelled at the woman, "shut up!"

"Sorry," mumbled Splat.

"Not you—her. How are you feeling?"

He turned to the woman. "How are you feeling?"

"Not her—you."

"Me?" He looked down at his shoulders, which were covered with bits of glass. "Dandruff. Bad dandruff." That's when I knew he was okay.

One of the mall security guards had been standing nearby when the incident happened. He helped us to our feet and told us what he'd seen—the trash bin rolling toward the listening booth, apparently under its own power, and then the crash.

Obviously it was just an accident. The bin just happened to start moving across the floor. It just happened to head straight for our booth. And all this just happened to occur only an hour after Cranston and Formica had seen us following them.

The medics arrived a moment later and checked us over for cuts. Splat had some on the backs of his arms and on his neck, but nothing serious.

"You were lucky," one of the medics said as he pressed a bandage into place. "Your hair and clothes took the brunt of it."

"That wasn't luck," I said. "He always coats himself with a protective layer of grease. The glass slid off."

"The real danger with flying glass," the other medic told me, "is getting it in your face and eyes. If he hadn't been covering you, there's no telling what kind of injuries you would have gotten."

How do you go about thanking a person you've just insulted? "Splat—"

"You don't have to say anything, Sizzle. What do words mean, anyway?" He shrugged. "Myself, I prefer sexual favors."

The medics left, and we spoke with the police, who had arrived in the meantime to make a report. Like the security guard, they'd been able to find no indication of how the trash bin had started rolling. None of the witnesses had seen anything suspicious, and dusting the bin for fingerprints revealed nothing. In their report the police labeled the whole thing an accident. We asked them to give a copy to Denton, then headed home.

I made three phone calls later that afternoon.

"Hello."

"Is this Lane Weatherby?"

"Yes, it is."

"You sound a little out of breath."

"I just got home and had to run for the phone. Who is this?"

"Prudence Szyznowski. Do you remember me?"

"Yes, I'm afraid I do."

"That's odd. We've only spoken once. Or have we met more recently?"

"No, we haven't. I just happen to have a good memory for names, especially of people who've been rude to me. How did you get my phone number?"

"Something called a telephone book. Mr. Weatherby, where were you this afternoon?"

"That's none of your business."

"Does the word *garbage* ring a bell?"

"I beg your pardon?"

"Never mind. I just thought I might have seen you this afternoon at the Santa Monica Mall."

"I never go to the mall. It's a filthy, disgusting place—just the sort of place you'd like."

"Do you know William Cranston?"

"No, I don't And now if you'll excuse me, Miss Szyznowski, I have more important things to do. Good-bye."

"Hello, Anthony?"

"Yes."

"This is Sizzle."

"Oh. You heard everything, didn't you?"

Careful. "What do you mean?"

"You know—at the restaurant. William's plan to sabotage

89

the benefit concert: If I don't show up, the string section falls on its face, and the whole concert's a flop."

"That's his plan?"

"Yeah. I got to give the guy credit, it's clever. But I can't go through with it. That's what I'm going to tell him. The deal's off."

"Wasn't there more to it than that?"

"All right, so a little money changed hands. What were you doing following us, anyway?"

"I could ask you the same question."

"Huh?"

"An hour after you saw us in the restaurant, somebody pushed a trash bin into our listening booth at Arnie's."

"My God. Are you all right?"

"Yeah, no thanks to your friends."

His voice changed key, from an E-flat minor to a shrill F major. "Now wait a minute. I'd never get involved with something like that, and neither would William. He may want to get ahead, but he'd never hurt anybody. Besides, I was with him until two o'clock."

"What about his buddy with the wig?"

"Who do you mean?"

"Cranston's hit man."

"His *hit man*? Are you nuts?"

It was obvious he knew nothing about it. Anthony wasn't smart enough to lie, which was exactly the reason Cranston wouldn't have told him more than he needed to know.

"Okay, I believe you. But you're still a jerk for trying to sell the orchestra down the river."

"I told you, the deal's off. I'm calling William the minute we get off the phone."

"Good. Just one thing, Anthony."

"Yeah?"

"Don't mention the trash bin. I don't want Cranston getting upset."

"Denton here."

"This is Prudence Szyznowski. Did you get a copy of the police report?"

"You mean your accident over at the mall? Just got it. You okay?"

"Yeah, but it was no accident."

"The report says otherwise."

"It happened just an hour after we heard Cranston and Formica plotting to sabotage the orchestra. They saw us. There's got to be a connection."

"Listen, Szyznowski, will you stop playing detective? I warned you once. Now, I'm a busy man. We're following up some leads on the Brody case, and I can assure you they have nothing to do with Cranston or Linoleum."

"Formica."

"Whatever. Just do me a favor—stay home. And stop calling, huh?"

"Okay. I just want you to remember this conversation when Pauling and I are found at the bottom of the river wearing concrete Adidas."

"You got quite an imagination, Szyznowski."

"You don't. And that's the problem."

16

![checkered bar decoration]

"My young orchestra friends, a dress rehearsal is a thing of beauty. We are in our formal clothings. We are on top of the stage in the lovely Royce Hall auditorium at UCLA. We play all our musics from starting to ending just the way they should be. And for one last time before the concert begin, we don't playing for our audience but for each others. Please, let us try *Die Meistersinger,* and I want you now to think of your friends who be sitting around you. Play nice for them, yes? And play nice for me."

It was ten o'clock Saturday morning. The concert was just four hours away. Vidor Pirelli had given his usual dress-rehearsal speech. But the electricity of concert day just wasn't there. Oh, there was plenty of tension, but none of it had to do with Hans Kleiman's music or the Pirelli Youth

Orchestra. The only thing people were interested in was *after* the concert. Would the kidnappers keep their word and release Brody, or not? By comparison, the upcoming performance—even though it might be the orchestra's last —seemed pretty inconsequential.

The orchestra sounded terrible, but it was only partly because Brody was missing. Someone else was missing as well: Anthony Formica. Calls were placed to his home, but there was no answer.

Without their concertmaster, the violins limped through the Wagner, unsure of phrasing and badly in need of leadership. When Mr. Pirelli cut off the last note, he wiped his forehead with a handkerchief and flung it onto the podium. "Where please is Anthony? We needing our concertmaster this minute."

The next piece was a Mozart symphony that didn't require trumpet or tuba. "Mr. Pirelli," I said, "Arthur and I could go to Anthony's house and check on him."

"Prudence, thank you. And please to hurry."

After stowing our instruments in the warm-up room backstage, we jumped into the Packard and took off for Formica's house. It was about a ten-minute drive, and on the way we discussed what we would do to him if he had gone back on his word and cooperated with Cranston. I'd rather not go into the details, but it involved a violin and a vat of acid.

As we approached the canyon road where Anthony lived, a familiar car pulled out in front of us. "The green Buick!" Splat said. He hunched over the wheel, and I could see an Indy 500 gleam in his eye.

"Don't speed up," I said. "We don't want him to notice us. Besides, I think I know where he's going."

We hung back, keeping as low a profile as we could in a

car that was six feet tall. Just as I suspected, the Buick continued up the street toward Anthony's house. Either Anthony had been lying to me on the phone and already knew who Mr. X was, or he was about to find out. As the car neared Anthony's driveway, we waited for it to slow down.

It never did.

"Something's wrong here," I said.

"Yeah—you."

We drove past Anthony's house, staying a block or so behind the Buick. It crossed Sunset Boulevard and headed into Beverly Hills, where it turned south on Rodeo Drive. Apparently Mr. X hadn't spotted us, because he was barely going thirty miles an hour. At the end of the second block he slowed down and pulled up to the curb. We parked nearby.

The man who stepped out of the Buick was indeed the familiar broad-shouldered form of Mr. X, wearing a blazer, tie, and slacks. But when he turned around, we got a shock.

"Hey, it's not Weatherby!" I said.

"Then who is it?"

"I don't know, but let's stay with him." We got out of the car. "Try to look inconspicuous."

"Sure. Just another couple of kids in formal evening attire."

There was enough foot traffic so we could stay close without being seen. Up ahead, Mr. X strolled leisurely down the sidewalk, stopping every once in a while to window-shop. When he window-shopped, we window-shopped. The fact that we weren't always next to a window didn't seem to bother anybody.

He made purchases at a jewelry store and a luggage shop, then went into an exclusive men's clothing store. "I'm getting a definite feeling about this," Splat said as we inspected the bricks on a nearby building.

"About the bricks?"

"About our friend with the wig. My feeling is that Mr. X has just made or is about to make a big wad of money."

"What's the luggage for?"

"Either to put the money in, or to leave town."

"How could there be money if there's no ransom?"

"That's what I can't figure out."

As Splat considered the matter, Mr. X left the store carrying yet another package. He locked the purchases in the trunk of his car, then went up the street to a Mercedes dealership. A salesman guided him to the most expensive model.

"Now I know he's got money," Splat said. "Mercedes salesmen have built-in rich detectors. This one's needle just went off the scale."

"I want to hear what they're saying. Maybe we can learn Mr. X's real name."

We drifted onto the perimeter of the lot and with our backs to Mr. X began moving from car to car, pretending to inspect each while at the same time edging closer and closer to our quarry.

"May I help you?" said a voice from behind us.

I started to turn around, but Splat gripped my arm in warning. "I wonder if you'd mind coming around on this side of us," he said. "We both have stiff necks—just came from a Ping-Pong tournament."

The man moved into view from our left, eyeing our clothes. "May I show you something?"

"Just browsing," I said. "We don't really need a sales-man."

The man stiffened. "Salesman? I'm a consumer consul-tant."

"What's that?" I asked.

"A salesman with a vest," Splat said.

"What is it you're looking for?" the man asked.

I peeked over my shoulder, and suddenly what we were looking for was walking right toward us, on his way out of the car lot. I flung open the door and jumped into the Mercedes, trying to pull Splat in after me. "Great car!" I said. "Check this interior." But Splat was still outside. Mr. X looked right at him and walked on without even blinking. Relieved, I sagged against the steering wheel. The horn let out a blast. Mr. X turned around for a second, then smiled and kept going.

"Perhaps you should leave," said our consumer consul-tant.

"My thought exactly," I said.

Mr. X went back to his car and drove down Wilshire Boulevard toward Westwood.

"I can't believe he didn't recognize me," Splat said as we followed.

"Must have been the tuxedo."

"Plus my complexion's improved."

"Right."

Up ahead, the Buick turned on Glendon, then skirted Westwood Village and went around a bend toward one of the most exclusive residential sections of West Los Angeles. As it went over a rise, a house came into view—a two-story English house, a house we were both familiar with. It be-longed to Frieda Kleiman.

"My God, he's going after her now," I said.

"Wearing a tie and blazer?"

"She's over seventy years old, Splat. It wouldn't take much to subdue her."

"Wait a second. Didn't she act strange when we talked to her, like she was scared?"

"Yeah. So?"

"Don't we know that she's rich? And that she's very fond of her nephew, Buckminster Brody?"

"Wow, there *is* a ransom. Mr. X is getting payoffs from her in exchange for Brody's safety. Poor Mrs. Kleiman. First her husband dies, and now this."

"So Cranston's not in on it. I hate to say this, but Denton was right. It was money after all."

"Hold on. If it was just money, why didn't Mr. X want Kleiman's piece to be played? Why did he steal my music? It doesn't fit."

The Buick turned into the Kleiman driveway. "Let's find out," Splat said.

We parked on a side street and sneaked through a hedge into the backyard. The lights were on in the drawing room, and we went up to the window.

Inside, Frieda Kleiman was just signing a check and handing it to Mr. X. But there was something wrong. She didn't look scared. In fact, she was smiling.

There was a sharp pain at the back of my head, and everything went black.

17

The lights went on. A few feet away, Splat stood with his hand on the switch. "Pinball, anyone?"

We were in the game room. I hadn't noticed on my first visit, but besides there being no windows, there was only one door. Splat tried it and found it locked.

"I don't get it," I said. "Who hit us over the head?"

"I have a hunch we won't find out until we know who Mr. X is. But I think I know who *didn't* do it—Cranston or Formica. This seems to go way beyond youth orchestras."

"Do you think Mrs. Kleiman's behind it?"

"She seems to be paying the bills."

I rubbed the back of my head. It felt like somebody'd been using it to play bumper pool. "When did you come to?" I asked.

"A few minutes ago—same as you. The sound of that car leaving must have woken us both up."

"Think we're alone?"

"Yeah. Other than the pounding in my ears, everything seems quiet."

I got unsteadily to my feet and looked around. "I feel like I've been out for hours. What time is it?"

"One o'clock. The concert starts in an hour."

"We've got to get out before they come back," I said.

"God, I wish I'd thought of that."

"Hey, stop joking around and let's figure this thing out."

"What's to figure? The door's locked. We're stuck."

"I can't accept that." Ten minutes later, after checking every corner and niche, I accepted it. Hans Kleiman had designed a game room and inadvertently built a prison. I flopped down on the piano bench next to Splat.

"Why would Mrs. Kleiman want to stop the premiere of her husband's last piece?" he asked. "You think she hated him?"

"No, I saw them together. She loved him, I'm sure of it. At least, I *was* sure of it."

"Maybe it had to do with money, like Denton said."

"She's rich. Look at this house. She doesn't need money."

"You sure?"

"Well, no," I admitted. "But what does money have to do with the concerto?"

"There was some money involved—the prize for solving the cryptogram."

"You're suggesting she'd do all this for five hundred dollars?"

"So maybe she's a little tightfisted."

There were several moments of silence while we studied the finish on the piano. "I keep coming back to that cryptogram," Splat said. "It's the one really unusual feature of Kleiman's piece."

" 'Look not to words, but to music; its mysteries are deeper, its rewards far greater.' "

"Good memory."

"Good friend. Hey, Splat, what if he meant the message literally, not figuratively."

"Huh?"

" 'Its mysteries are deeper'—maybe there's another puzzle, a harder one, in the music itself. 'Its rewards far greater' —maybe there's a second reward, much bigger than five hundred dollars, for whoever solves the music puzzle."

"Wow," he said, "a huge reward. That would explain why Mrs. Kleiman didn't want the concerto played—she wanted the money for herself!"

"But I'm sure Kleiman would have left her enough money."

"Funny word, *enough*. Means different things to different people." He looked around at our carpeted prison. "If we just had a copy of the concerto . . ."

"I've got one with me."

"Where?"

"Same place I was carrying the message—in my head." I leaned over the keyboard and plunked out the theme of Kleiman's concerto.

"So you think that's a puzzle of some kind?" he asked.

"Maybe. It was going to be printed in the program notes." I got a pencil and paper from one of the tables and wrote down first the musical notes, then under them their letter equivalents: D E B A D D B G E A F F.

"That's it!" said Splat. "Debaddbgeaff!"

"Gesundheit. You know, if you were trying to leave a message using musical notes, the biggest problem would be having just the first several letters of the alphabet to work with—*a* through *g*. Which is fine as long as the message is about a cab or a bed or a bead. But what if it's not?"

"I'd call Western Union."

"Or maybe you'd do this." I wrote the letters of the alphabet, and under them I put the letters *A* through *G* as many times as they would fit.

A B C D E F G H I J K L M N O P Q R S T U V W X Y Z

A B C D E F G A B C D E F G A B C D E F G A B C D E

Splat nodded thoughtfully, then caught himself. "Hey, I'm supposed to be the cryptogram expert."

"I've been studying." Using the double row of letters as a guide, I went back to the top of the page and beneath Kleiman's letter-note equivalents wrote all the other letters that each note might possibly represent.

D E B A D D B G E A F F

K L I H K K I N L H M M

R S P O R R P U S O T T

Y Z W V Y Y W   Z V

"Reminds me of some soup I once ate," said Splat.

"Just look at it, wise guy, because our answer may be in there someplace. See any words that go left to right?"

"Yeah, *de park*. As in de park has flowers in de spring."

"Real good, Splat."

"Wait a second—*repay*. Let's see, repay rig soft. What do you think?"

"Little obscure, but nice try." Then I saw it. "*Reward!*"

"And there's *in*! He's giving directions."

"Reward in soft? That can't be right. Reward in . . . *loft!*"

101

"We got it!" cried Splat. "There *is* a big secondary reward—that's why Mrs. Kleiman didn't want the concerto played! Now the only question is, where's the loft?"

"I hate to be a wet blanket, but this room not only has no loft, it has no windows."

"Yeah, but we figured out the message! And you know what? The loft has to be somewhere in this house. I'm sure Kleiman hid the reward himself, and he was too sick to travel." Agitated, Splat went to the door and gave it an inch-by-inch inspection, looking for a crack or a weakness of some kind.

While he did, I absently fingered the melody of Kleiman's concerto. "We'll batter down the door, that's all," Splat was murmuring. "We need something big to ram it with." He looked around, and his gaze came to rest on the piano.

"Forget it," I said, "this is a Steinway grand. You have any idea how much this thing's worth?"

Splat grasped the flesh on his arm. "You have any idea how much *this* thing's worth? Mr. X could come back any minute wanting to play Bach fugues on my head."

"Listen, I know the piano's big, but—" I looked at the door, then at the concert grand. Over my head, a hundred watts blinked on. "Splat, how did they get this piano into the room?"

"We're about to die, and you're interested in furniture moving techniques?"

"There's no way they could have used that door. The stairway leading down from the next floor is too cramped for a concert grand—not to mention these big pinball machines and video games."

"There's got to be another door!" Splat exclaimed. "Sizzle, whatever I said about you, I take it back. Well, most of it."

We knew the other door was there, if we just looked hard enough. And sure enough, an hour later, Splat located a switch on the wall behind the dartboard. He put his hand on it, then turned to me. "I have a sudden vision of us plunging into a tank full of alligators."

"Pull the switch."

He closed his eyes and yanked.

The surface next to the dartboard began to move. When it stopped, there was an opening ten feet wide leading directly onto the driveway. It was perfect. Hans Kleiman had designed his game room so that even the walls contained a puzzle.

I started for the door. "Come on—the concert should still be going, and Denton'll be there."

"But now's our chance to find the loft."

"Wrong. Now's our chance to escape before they show up again. There'll be plenty of time later to come back with the police and find the loft."

"And if Mr. X finds it first?"

"Don't worry, he hasn't solved the code. If he had, he wouldn't still be holding Brody."

We heard a car drive up.

"I have a sudden urge to go to the concert," said Splat.

We sprinted out the door, then climbed into the Packard and tore off down the street.

"Want a pizza?" I said.

"Will you stop with the food?"

"That car just reminded me of it."

"What car?"

"The one parked next door to the Kleimans' house. The one we heard drive up. The one with CLANCY's PIZZA painted on the side."

18

The parking lot in front of the auditorium was full, so we left the Packard under some trees across the street. Inside the musicians' entrance were two uniformed police officers, plus Detective Denton.

"We know who did it," I told him as we rushed past.

Vidor Pirelli was just leaving the wings to begin the final piece of the concert. "Tell him to stall," Splat yelled to a stagehand as we hurried to get our instruments. We entered the backstage warm-up room where we had left them.

There, half hidden behind Splat's tuba, was Buckminster Brody. He was bound and gagged, and when he saw us his eyes bulged with excitement.

While Splat untied the ropes on Brody's wrists and ankles, I took off his gag. "Mr. Brody, are you okay?" I asked.

"Y-Yes, I seem to be well, that is, fine, that is—oh, Prudence, it's so good to see you. I thought I might not see anyone again."

"Holy mackerel," someone said behind us. Niles Denton stood in the doorway.

"Stick with us, Denton," said Splat. "You might learn something."

"But—"

"We'll explain everything after the concert," I said, taking my trumpet out of the case.

Onstage, Pirelli was doing his best to stall. "So you see, my fine ladies and gentlemens," he said to the audience, "Sibelius write very great music which for many years was known only in his own shores. Now he belong to the world. How many of you have listen to his musics?"

In the tenth row, a gray-haired woman raised her hand. It was Frieda Kleiman. Sitting next to her was Mr. X.

"I guess they just wanted to make sure the concerto wasn't on the program," said Splat.

That's when it hit me. "Tell the police not to let either of them get away. They can be arrested after the concert." I ran onstage, huddled for a moment with Pirelli, then hurried to the stage door.

"Where are you going?" Splat called as I went past.

"I'm doing a favor for an old friend," I replied. "I'll be right back."

I raced across campus to the rehearsal room. Using Pirelli's keys, I unlocked a metal cabinet and pulled out the music to the Kleiman Trumpet Concerto.

It took only a minute to hand out the parts, but during that time the buzzing from the audience was growing louder and louder. As Splat took his seat in the orchestra, Pirelli raised his hand for silence.

"Kind friends, thank you so very much on your patience," he said. "We having a surprise for you today, a wonderful treat that make us all very happy. Instead of the Second Symphony of Mr. Sibelius, we now present to you the Trumpet Concerto of our late friend Hans Kleiman. Since we are sight-reading, please forgive some few mistakes." There was excited comment in the audience. "Our soloist is our own Miss Prudence Szyznowski. Please, Prudence."

I set up my stand next to the podium. As I adjusted it, I checked the audience, and there in the front row was my dad, clearly relieved to see me.

Behind me someone whispered, "Good luck." It was Anthony.

"Where were you this morning?" I hissed.

He fingered his violin nervously. "Cranston called again. It took me a while to convince him I really meant no, so I was late to the dress rehearsal. I'm sorry."

"Say that with your fiddle. We'll need it in this concerto." He nodded.

A moment later, Pirelli gave the downbeat, and the music began. The cellos were first, with a low, murmuring phrase that wove back and forth in a pattern. Over that, the woodwinds trilled and the brass and tympani pulsed. As they crescendoed, I brought the trumpet to my lips, took a deep breath, and played. It was the initial statement of the theme, which in this opening movement was almost a question, asked by someone who is troubled or confused. As the movement went on, the orchestra took up the question and added its own nuances, sometimes hurt, sometimes resigned, sometimes angry. We had never rehearsed the concerto, but today that seemed to be working to our advantage. Everyone was concentrating intently on his own part, listening to the others, discovering the music as it was played. Whenever the group faltered, Anthony would forge ahead, leading by example.

The second movement was a romp. My part skipped over the top of the orchestra like a stone across a brook, and the effect couldn't have been more different from the first movement. It was as if the opening question had been set aside for a few moments of fun. The string section plucked a happy *pizzicato* melody, while the flutes and clarinets noodled cheerfully. I could almost see Hans Kleiman sitting in his downstairs room, playing a game of checkers or Parcheesi. There was a somber note or two toward the end, but the overall feeling was one of optimism.

The final movement began with unaccompanied trumpet. The opening question was raised once again, then the orchestra joined in with new comments, some of them from the second movement. Music and games were Hans Kleiman's two great loves, and here I thought I could hear him trying to combine and make sense of them. Could either of them answer the concerto's opening question? Halfway through the movement, in my solo part, Kleiman gave his answer: a repeat of the original theme, but now as a statement rather than a question. As the piece drew to a close, the theme was picked up by the low brass, then the woodwinds, and finally the strings and percussion. Then, just as it neared a climax, there was a sudden stillness—three beats of absolute silence—and out of the calm I played the theme once through, all alone, very quietly.

I'd practiced the passage before, but this time, with the cryptogram fresh in my mind, a notation at the bottom of the page leaped out at me. Instead of the usual abbreviation *p*, Kleiman had gone to the trouble of marking the dynamics "*piano* = soft." I finished the theme, and the orchestra came back in for the final chords, but I barely heard them because fireworks were going off in my head. The Kleiman Trumpet Concerto had received its premiere—and in the process Hans Kleiman had told me where the reward was really hidden.

The auditorium erupted with applause, and beyond the bright footlights I could see the audience on its feet. I looked back at the orchestra, where Splat was grinning at me like he had just discovered the cure for acne.

"Prudence," Pirelli was saying, "they clapping for you." He took my hand, and together we bowed. When we straightened up, he beckoned into the darkened auditorium, and a moment later we were joined onstage by a very nervous Frieda Kleiman. The applause grew, and there were shouts of approval.

"What about my nephew?" she said to Pirelli. "Isn't this putting him in danger?"

Pirelli took her hand in both of his and turned to the audience. "Mrs. Kleiman, dear friends," he said, motioning for quiet, "I am please to announce that our dear Mr. Buckminster Brody is sound and safe."

There was a new burst of applause, and Mrs. Kleiman exclaimed, "Where? Where is he?"

"Backstage—you will see."

She leaned forward and hugged Pirelli with her free arm, and when she pulled back there were tears in her eyes. Then she faced outward and smiled, dipping her head in appreciation.

"You should be proud," I told her as the three of us bowed. "You're giving a better performance than I did."

"Pardon me?"

"I know you're surprised to see me—almost as surprised as I was to see you with your good buddy Mr. X, the guy with the wig and the blazer."

"Blazer? Oh, you mean Marcel Lombard, my attorney."

"He provides some very unusual legal services." Before she could answer, I headed for the wings.

Just offstage, Denton was waiting. "Okay, Szyznowski, it's time for you to tell me what's going on."

"There's something else I need to do first. In the meantime, just make sure Mrs. Kleiman and the man in the blazer don't get away."

The curtain next to us rustled, and Splat appeared, lugging his tuba. "Sizzle, you were incredible!"

"You're pretty incredible yourself. Come on, we've got one more job to finish." He set down his tuba and followed.

As we hurried across the street toward the trees where Splat had parked his car, I explained what I'd discovered during the piece. "There was one more clue in the music. It was right in my part: *piano* = soft. The reward's not in the loft, but in the 'soft'—in other words, the piano. We were right next to it in Hans Kleiman's game room."

"Thank you, Miss Szyznowski," said a voice behind us. We turned, and there holding a gun was Marcel Lombard. "The money would have reverted to Mrs. Kleiman in several days anyway, but now we can make sure no one else gets it in the meantime."

"The mysterious Mr. X," I said, my mind racing. "You look different without the mask."

"Yeah," Splat said, "you look better with it on. Nice wig, though."

I kept hoping for someone to notice us, but we'd parked

in an isolated area. "How did you get by the police?" I asked.

"I checked my escape routes before the concert. There was an emergency exit downstairs."

"You're very good," Splat said. "Too bad you didn't put your talent to use in a legitimate profession—say, law."

His right eyelid twitched. "I wish we could chat all afternoon, but I'm afraid if we stay too much longer someone may discover us."

"Don't look," I said, "but here comes my father."

Lombard glanced over his shoulder for just an instant, and I lashed out with my foot. The gun went clattering off to the left, where I pounced on it and pointed it toward Lombard.

"I told you not to look," I said.

Splat moved over behind me. "Shall we stroll back to the auditorium? I'm sure the police will be glad to see Mr. Lombard."

Lombard looked past us. "It's about time you got here," he said, as if speaking to someone else. "Keep them covered."

"Come on, Lombard," I said. "That's the oldest trick in the book."

A voice came from behind us. "Drop your gun, that is, pistol, uh, revolver. Please."

19

Tell me Tchaikovsky was tone-deaf. Tell me Columbus was afraid of the water. Tell me J. Paul Getty couldn't balance his checkbook. But don't tell me Buckminster Brody would ever hold a gun on anybody. It's just too ridiculous.

I dropped the weapon I was holding, and Lombard picked it up.

"Prudence, you don't know how much this upsets me," Brody said.

"I'm not crazy about it myself."

"Lombard kidnapped you," Splat said. "He hit you over the head—I saw it."

Brody rubbed behind one ear. "He convinced me it was

111

necessary to what we were doing. A sacrifice to the cause, you might say."

"Money," I said. "Great cause."

"You're the one who knocked us out, aren't you?" asked Splat.

"I regret, uh, I'm afraid so. Marcel telephoned and told me you were following him."

I turned to Lombard. "You knew?"

"You couldn't have been more obvious at the car dealer if you'd brought your entire orchestra."

"But how could you have called Brody? You didn't stop at a phone."

"I have one in my car."

"So," Splat said, "this nasty little composition wasn't a duet, but a trio—Lombard, Kleiman, and Brody."

"Frieda Kleiman?" laughed Lombard. "She had no more to do with it than you did."

"But we saw her paying you off," I said. "And she didn't want to talk to us about her husband's music."

"She was writing me a check for a legal fee. After all, I'm her attorney. As for not cooperating, would you talk if you were getting phone calls from a kidnapper threatening to kill your favorite nephew?"

Splat looked over at Brody. "How did you get us into the game room without her noticing?"

"Marcel kept her occupied with business while I used the secret entrance you seem to have found. It can be opened from the outside by key. A few minutes later, the two of them went to a nice long preconcert meal, that is, luncheon. I stayed with you for a couple of hours, then went to get some food for myself."

"So you could show up at the auditorium near the end of the concert," Splat said, "in time for Lombard to tie you up in a backstage room. You thought nobody'd find you till the performance was over."

"We were wrong, uh, mistaken, about that," said Brody, "but everything seems to have worked out splendidly, don't you agree?"

Lombard glanced toward the auditorium, where the crowd was beginning to spill out onto the parking lot. "Time to go, kiddies. Mr. Brody's getting in your car with you, and you'll do exactly as he says. I'll be right behind."

"Doggone it," exclaimed Splat, "I forgot my tuba. I'd better go get it."

"Don't bother," Lombard said. "Where you're going, you won't need a tuba. Ever."

"How about a flute?"

"If I understand him correctly," I said, "a harp would be more like it."

"But I hate harps."

"Get in," said Lombard.

We pulled out of the lot, with Splat and me in the front seat and Brody in the back, holding the gun on us. Lombard followed in his Buick.

"We're going to Topanga Canyon," Brody said. "Take Sunset to the coast and turn right."

"What happens at Topanga Canyon?" Splat asked.

"I'm afraid you're going to have a mishap, that is, accident. That's why we're taking your car. Like you, it will suffer some damage."

"You're not really going to kill us, are you?" I said.

"I don't want to. But I will."

"Just for some money?"

"Prudence, money is odd. When you have a lot of it, it's not important. When you have very little, it positively dominates you."

"I have very little, and it doesn't dominate me."

"It will. Just wait till you grow older. I mean . . . oh, sorry."

"I thought you had plenty of money," said Splat.

"Yes, I *had* plenty, but it's almost gone. I need the money from my aunt's estate—"

"Of course!" I exclaimed. "Why didn't we think of that?"

"Think of what?" asked Splat.

"We were right about the music puzzle, and the secondary prize, and the fact that greed was the motive behind this whole thing. But it wasn't Mrs. Kleiman's greed; it was her nephew's. He stood to inherit the reward money eventually if nobody solved the puzzle."

"How much are we talking about here?" Splat asked Brody.

"One million dollars—half of Hans Kleiman's two million dollar estate. You see, Uncle Hans told Lombard he'd hidden a bank draft for a million dollars, made out to the Pirelli Youth Orchestra, but he didn't tell him where. He didn't tell anyone, not even Aunt Frieda. The only way to find the draft was to solve the puzzle—the *second* puzzle—and we couldn't figure it out. The draft expires in seven days, that is, one week from today, so if no one finds the solution, the money reverts to his estate."

"Why didn't he just *give* the money to the orchestra?" Splat asked. "Why take the chance we wouldn't get it?"

I suddenly realized I knew why. "It was part of what he believed. He told me it's the possibility of losing that makes winning worthwhile. Otherwise it wouldn't have been a game."

"I see," Splat said. "And if the orchestra loses, Brody wins —as soon as Aunt Frieda kicks off. Tell me, Mr. Brody, are you going to kill her, too?"

"Don't talk like that!" he snapped. "I love Aunt Frieda, and she loves me. She'll leave me, I mean will me, her entire estate when she passes away."

"What if she crosses you up and lives another twenty years?" Splat asked. "Love only goes so far."

"We don't have to talk about this," Brody said. "I'm the one holding the gun."

We turned north on Pacific Coast Highway. To our left was a splendid view, perhaps our last, of the ocean.

"I never figured you to be the violent type, Mr. Brody," I said.

"I'm not. This whole scheme, that is, project, got completely out of hand. At first we were just going to vandalize the rehearsal room. When Pirelli insisted on playing Uncle Hans's piece anyway, we came up with the idea of kidnapping. Since it involved some risk for Marcel, I agreed to give him a third of the million dollars, rather than the original tenth, plus of course his attorney's fees for handling the estate. The only person who was going to be hurt, uh, injured, was me, when he hit me over the head."

"Then we chased him that day after interviewing your wife," I said.

Brody nodded. "That was the turning point, at least as far as Marcel was concerned. Once you could recognize his car, he was in danger of being discovered. I tried, that is, attempted, to persuade him to get a new car, but Marcel, being the kind of person he is, felt threats would work better."

"So he wrecked my trumpet and left a note."

"Yes, but there was a problem, I mean, dilemma. He found the score, the trumpet part, and the cryptogram in your case. We hadn't dreamed there were other copies. Since the whole idea of the kidnapping scheme, uh, plan, was to prevent anyone from playing the game, Marcel was thrown into a panic. He would deny it, but that was un-doubtedly his reaction, and it explains why he made his next major mistake."

"The shooting," Splat said.

"Correct. Just to make sure you were frightened off the case, he fired some shots—making sure, of course, to miss. When he told me about it, I was very angry because I wanted to avoid even the slightest chance we might hurt someone, and because the noise could easily have attracted the police."

"He didn't listen to you, did he?" I said.

"Marcel doesn't listen to anyone."

"Talk about making noise and attracting the police," I said, "what about the shopping mall? He was lucky he wasn't caught."

Brody nodded. "He knew you'd been following Formica and Cranston and felt an attack at that time would convince you they were guilty and throw you completely off our scent. Obviously he was wrong."

"Oh, but he wasn't," I said. "We *were* convinced. But then we just happened to see his car again this morning and followed it to Mrs. Kleiman's house."

"It was just a coincidence?" croaked Brody. "I told him to get another car."

"He was on his way to do that," said Splat. "He was looking for a new Mercedes—about a week too late."

"Here's Topanga Canyon," Brody said. "Turn right."

"You didn't want to see anyone get hurt, but now you're going to murder us," I said.

"He's just an all-or-nothing kind of guy," Splat said.

Brody tensed. "I'm a very kind, I mean, gentle, person. I don't want to do this, but you've forced me to."

116

Suddenly I knew that Buckminster Brody, good old Mr. Brody, could never go through with killing anyone. "Give me the gun, Mr. Brody," I said, trying to keep my voice from shaking. I held out my hand, palm up, and moved it toward him.

"Don't, Prudence," he said, his knuckles white on the handle of the revolver. As I reached farther over the seat, he began to blink. My hand was a yard away from the gun, then a foot, then a half foot, and Brody was growing more frantic by the inch. "I'm warning you, Prudence," he begged. "Don't come any closer or I'll have to shoot."

"You're too nice a man, Mr. Brody. You won't shoot."

There was a deafening explosion, and something whizzed past the left side of my head. "So I was wrong," I said.

"You maniac!" screamed Splat. "You fired a gun in my car!" While I checked my hand and face for missing parts, Splat scanned the interior of the Packard for damage of a much more serious nature. "The bullet must have gone through the open window. You're a very lucky man, Mr. Brody."

At the sound of the gunshot, Lombard had pulled his Buick up close behind us to see what was wrong. Brody waved him off. As he turned back to us, I saw that his face was flushed. The explosion had catapulted him into a land of blood and power, and he appeared to be enjoying it. "*I'm* lucky? You're lucky, both of you, to be alive. And as for this jalopy, this junk heap, you could set off a grenade in here and never notice the damage."

With Brody's last sentence, a terrible calm settled over Splat. He glanced into the rearview mirror, then deliberately buckled his seat belt. Splat never buckles his seat belt. I decided I'd better fasten mine.

Topanga Canyon Road is a narrow strip of pavement that winds precariously above a deep, rocky gorge. Traffic heading away from the ocean travels in the outside lane for much of the trip, so that a passenger looking out his window sees only Topanga Creek hundreds of yards below. That tiny ribbon of water was what I was staring at when I felt the car begin to accelerate.

It was so gradual that at first Brody didn't notice it. Soon, though, we were swaying as we rounded corners. "Hey, slow down," he said.

"Don't worry," Splat replied. "Junk heaps can't go very fast." The engine hummed effortlessly as the speedometer edged past 40 to 45.

Behind us, the Buick began to honk. Brody looked over his shoulder, then at Splat. "I said, slow down."

"Mr. Brody, this car's twice as old as I am. Do you honestly think that Buick can't keep up?" The speedometer needle crossed 50. The car was whipping around curves, its body staying surprisingly level.

The Buick was indeed keeping up, but it was rocking badly going into turns. I could see Lombard wrestling the steering wheel, his mouth wide open in a bellow of rage.

"Slow down! Slow down!" yelled Brody.

"No," said Splat. His mouth was set in a hard, straight line, and in his eyes was the same look of concentration he got when playing the tuba.

Brody placed the barrel of the gun on Splat's head. "If you don't you'll be very sorry."

"Mr. Brody," I said, "never shoot the driver. That's the first thing they teach you in driver ed."

We skidded around another curve. The Buick followed, tipping almost onto two wheels. When it straightened out, the honking started again. Splat looked in the rearview mirror and clucked his tongue. "Those new Buicks have a bad suspension system. Nice horn, though."

The gun was shaking in Brody's hand. A sign loomed in front of us. It showed an arrow doubled back to the left, and below that it said 15 mph.

"Now you've got to slow down!" shouted Brody.

"Second the motion," I said.

Splat edged the car as near the right shoulder of the road as he could. Then, without reducing his speed, he began the turn. He crossed over into the oncoming traffic lane to cut the corner. Leaning to his left, he swept the steering wheel around in a counterclockwise motion.

"No, no, no!" Brody cried, bracing himself against the door.

The car began to skid, at first just a bit, then more and more violently, back into the right-hand lane and toward the edge of the road, beyond which there was only a low railing and empty sky. For a crazy moment I could hear my dad telling me always to steer in the direction of a skid. I'd always wondered exactly what that meant, and now Splat demonstrated. He spun the steering wheel to the right, and the rear wheels tried to dig in. They drifted off the pavement and onto the dirt, spinning furiously. I looked out the window and could see no road, no fence, no nothing. There was a bump, and suddenly we were around the curve and heading down the highway.

"Saved by the guardrail," said Splat.

"Ghrhgg," commented Brody, his face a pale mint-green.

I looked past him out the rear window just in time to see the Buick splinter the railing and plunge into the canyon. Brody saw it, too. "Stop this car!" he screamed.

"Okay," Splat said. He jammed on the brakes, and Brody was thrown against the front seat. When his wrist hit, the gun flew from his hand onto the seat between Splat and me. I picked it up and pointed it toward Brody, who was just scrambling to sit up.

"That's the second thing they teach you in driver ed," I said. "Always fasten your seat belt."

A traffic cop rounded the corner behind us, his light flashing.

Postlude

"Well, Sizzle, what do you think?"

"I think I should have stayed home."

"Hey, come on. We cracked the kidnapping case and saved the orchestra at the same time. Don't you believe in celebrating?"

"This isn't my idea of celebrating."

"You got something against drive-ins?"

"It's just not what I pictured when you said 'a night on the town.' Splat, I'm wearing a formal gown."

"So it's a sophisticated movie."

"*The Texas Chainsaw Massacre?*"

"Hey, some of the corpses were very well dressed. And when they caught the killer, they gave him a good-looking striped outfit."

"Like the one poor Mr. Brody's going to be wearing."

" 'Poor Mr. Brody'? Sizzle, the man tried to kill us."

"He was just upset."

"I was pretty upset myself. Anyway, if you have to feel sorry for somebody, make it Lombard. After a month in the hospital with broken legs and broken arms, prison will seem like summer camp. I guess that'll teach him to fool with us."

"Their mistake was fooling with Hans Kleiman. It was his game, and he played it perfectly."

"You played pretty well too, Sizzle. Kleiman's trumpet concerto got a great premiere, and the Pirelli Youth Orchestra got the million dollars that was hidden in the piano. You deserve something special—I don't know, a prize of some kind."

"Got anything in mind?"

"As a matter of fact, yes."

"Splat, why are you sliding across the seat toward me?"

"I'm bringing you your prize."

"I'm getting a bad feeling about this."

"Don't worry, you'll like it."

"Splat—"

"Now, see? That wasn't so bad, was it?"

"Mm. No it wasn't. In fact, I wouldn't mind another one."

"One more onion ring, coming right up."

"You're a good friend, Splat."

"This one's kind of greasy. Want some ketchup on it?"

"No, I like it just the way it is."